AF470689

MEMOIRS
OF A
TWELFTH MAN

MEMOIRS OF A TWELFTH MAN

The recollections of J.A.P. Withers of Stripford Rural Cricket Club

ANTHONY COUCH

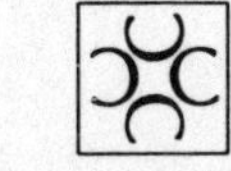

THE CROWOOD PRESS

First published in 1984 by
THE CROWOOD PRESS
Crowood House Ramsbury
Marlborough
Wiltshire SN8 2HE

British Library Cataloguing in Publication Data

Couch, Anthony
Memoirs of a twelfth man.
I. Title
823'.914 [F] PR6053.07/

ISBN 0–946284–35–0

Set in 11 on 14 point Plantin
by Inforum Ltd, Portsmouth
Printed in Great Britain
by The Pitman Press, Bath

To Oliver and Humphrey

Contents

MEMOIRS
OF A
TWELFTH MAN

Preface

When I was asked to write a few prefatory words to this book, I replied 'Good wine needs no bush'. Then it was pointed out that foreigners might get their hands on it, or tennis players, and it was suggested that I should picture a Greek person, female, age fifty-two, with three sons in the Department of Antiquities. I immediately saw what everyone was getting at.

There is a similar game that is also called cricket. It is played on a larger, flatter field and all the equipment conforms to the Laws. But the big difference between the two games lies in the people who play them. Proper cricket is played by men who get paid for doing so, or believe they're good enough to be. Village cricket is played by people who should be paid not to. All professions and trades are represented in village cricket, except the profession of cricketer.

Village cricket is played on a flattish field in or near a village. It requires two teams of eleven players (more or less), six stumps, two bats and a ball. The object of the game is to score more runs than your opponents, and that's it. That's cricket.

Village cricket is to Englishmen what the balalaika is to Russians: a device for escaping into a make-believe world where one's niceness is rewarded by figures of 6 for 18. In this world there are no cow pats in the exact spot the skipper's placed you. The ball is always red and round, and always finds the meat of the bat. No matter how often one's expectations turn to dust, there's always a chance that today you'll play at least one good stroke or actually hold a catch. The sun beams down, one's friends keep shouting 'Well hit', and there is a mischievous strawberry jam sponge for tea served by a girl with laughing brown eyes.

Fantasy, of course. So why does one do it? Because cricket is, I believe, the most difficult game to arrange and play ever invented. Making that first phone call in the dead of winter ('Is that you, Jack? I say, we're arranging a match against Grimhook, August 29th . . .') is like shaking one's fist in the faces of the Gods. Often it rains, or the other team gets lost, or your kit has vanished, or your flannels have got a funny purple stain right down the front. Or, worst of all, the damn'd farmer has forgotten to take the cows out of the field. A doings with a crust is not good; one without a crust is simply frightful.

But each Spring, when I take my shirt and flannels off their wire hanger and lay them on the bed, I say to myself 'They can keep their bull-fighting and their mountain railways. They can keep their greasy food, over-weight sopranos and Louis Quinze furniture. I'm off to play cricket.'

And I go. I'm not brilliant. I don't possess a pair of pads any more. Often I find myself watching rather than playing these days or billed as twelfth man, but, like the lady in the painting, I'm there if needed.

As he leafs through the following pages, I hope the reader will catch a little of what I've experienced over the years – laughter, tears, fury, and a shocking throb in the right shoulder where Alfie Maltravers hit me with a short one. No matter whether you are sweating under an Arabian sky or freezing to death in South Shields, just remember: the old game is still played, the old Laws are still strictly observed (or totally ignored, as the case may be), corruption, vanity and downright incompetence still stalk the rain-washed pitches of England, and there are still only left-handed batting gloves in the bag.

*J. A. P. Withers,**
Legwell-over-Stripford

* Author of *Up the Garden Path, Discipline in the Garden* and *Up the Garden Path Again.*

I

My Greatest Innings

I'm not conceited about my cricket, any more than I'm conceited about my sense of humour. I have a certain inclination in both these areas, but I'm not alone in this. Hundreds of others are the same. I have a natural gift for Provençale cookery, too, but that is nothing to get big-headed about. Just think of all the people in the world, many of them women, who are every bit as good as I am. All right, they may not be natural comedians, and I daresay very few of them can play the spinners the way I do; but, for Heaven's sake, why should they?

I enjoy my cricket. I've had more than my share of fun and good fortune out in the middle. But I'm not going to pretend that literature's gain was cricket's loss. It's possible, I suppose, that I could have had a few seasons at the county level, maybe even have got representative honours, but a man has to decide where his true interests lie, in which field he can make the most telling contribution.

It was when my early poem 'Squeamish Tortoise' was accepted for publication by *The Listener* that I made the difficult decision to treat cricket simply as a pastime. I would continue to turn out for Stripford, once quite a good club side, but no longer would they own me, body and soul. From now on they would have to be content with what was left over after I'd squeezed myself dry at my desk.

Looking back on the events of that late summer from the security of a successful middle age I can smile. Thank God I've kept my sense of humour. At the time it was anything but funny. First of all the secretary of the club removed my name from the list of members available for selection. I was furious. I had *not* declared my unavailability. I had not been off-hand about Wednesday nets. I had not made tactless remarks about the fact that there were two Guestling-Knodes in the team, and *three* Boyd-Leathers! If a chap's good enough to play, then let him play, I say. If he's not, as was the case with most of the above-mentioned, well, who cares? It's only a game.

When I explained to the secretary, Hugh Boyd-Leathers, that I was under immense pressure from publishers and magazine editors he showed none of that quick warmth and barely-disguised envy one expects from the public. He claimed not to know what *The Listener* was, which I regarded as childish. He said he never read poetry – hardly a surprise! – and suggested I stuck to concrete gnomes. This last thrust was a reference to my mode of employment at that time, as a trainee manager in a landscape gardening business.

The basic nastiness of the man may be judged by the fact that several months later he stopped me outside the Grow Green Garden Emporium for the purpose of pointing out that he had scanned all the recent editions of *The Listener* but had failed to detect my poem. What sort of man is it who will go to all that trouble simply to be spiteful? I explained to him that 'Squeamish Tortoise' had been removed at the very last moment, with great reluctance, because of a diplomatic incident on the Belize border. This had interrupted the flow of wood pulp from the USSR, thus reducing the size of the periodical. Boyd-Leathers' expression of naked disbelief confirmed that he knew even less about foreign affairs than he did about the late cut, which will astonish those who have seen him flapping about outside the off-stump.

The reason I'm going on about Hugh Boyd-Leathers is because, by one of those odd quirks of fate, he was directly involved in the memorable innings I played at the end of that season. It was a good innings. Afterwards I realized it was the greatest I ever played, and H. B-L. was the spark that ignited the powder keg.

It was September, the last match of the season but one. Stripford were playing British Rail Manufacturing Sheds, Ingbury, a small plant that turned out those squiggly bits of iron that hold the rail on the sleeper. Stripford were confident of victory, and their offensively cocky attitude seemed justified when the railwaymen turned up two short.

Needless to say, I was no longer playing for the club. I will not be treated like a schoolboy by people who think that Christopher Isherwood bowls slow left arm for Kent. I had removed my name from the door of my steel locker and kicked the dust of the club room from my shoes. I had broken free; I was my own man again. The only reason I happened to be in the vicinity of the ground that Saturday was . . . well, idle curiosity really. Was it possible, I wondered, that I'd been replaced in the team by yet another Boyd-Leathers – Archie, a spotted youth and the youngest of the litter?

I chose to sit on one of the benches directly in front of the pavilion. I knew that my presence would irritate the secretary, and if he got his customary duck I'd be there, dominating his route back to the dressing-room. On the other hand, if he had one of those very rare days when he stumbled into double figures I could leave ostentatiously, as if bored to death by the slowness of the scoring.

However, I'd only been seated a few minutes when Andy

Guestling-Knode, our skipper – that is to say, the Stripford skipper – sidled up to me.

'Hullo, Gussy,' he said. 'Nice to see you.'

I let it pass. He obviously wanted something – an umpire or a fiver – but he wasn't going to get it from me.

'I wonder if you could help us out?' he said.

Ah, yes! Would I do a bit of scoring, perhaps, or make the tea.

'Thing is,' went on Guestling-Knode, 'the Ingbury chaps are a couple of chaps short. We've lent them young Archie, but they want one more. I suppose you wouldn't care to turn out for them, would you? Just to make up the numbers?'

Just to make up the numbers! That's what did it. Go in at No. 11 and field all day at deep third man. That's obviously what he had in mind. I saw red! As you will have deduced by now I'm a pretty easy-going sort of person. I don't take offence easily. But that was too much.

'Delighted!' I said, rising to my feet. 'Absolutely delighted.'

I gave him one of those looks usually reserved for sloppy dustmen and strode off to the visitors' dressing-room.

The Ingbury skipper was a short man with glasses, about forty-five. He didn't impress me as the sort of person who might be a cricketer, but I discovered later that he was a regular reader of *The Atlantic Review* and *The Nato Quarterly* which immediately put him into a different class from the riff-raff in the home dressing-room.

'Very kind of you to help us out,' he said. 'Where do you like to bat?'

'I normally open,' I said, 'but put me down at four or five. I don't want to upset your order.'

I have to confess that this was a slight warping of the truth. For Stripford I usually went in at eight where a sudden surge of runs from an aggressive batsman can completely change the shape of a match. On a number of occasions I've turned defeat into victory by knocking up a quick thirty – or so – coming in late. It's a sound tactic to save up one of your more reliable batsmen for an onslaught when the bowlers are tired. But on this particular Saturday I didn't want to be left with the sweepings of the railway sheds. I had work to do, and I needed room to do it.

Stripford batted first and, because the engine drivers hadn't got a decent bowler amongst them, managed to scrape together 194. I had a couple of overs late on – the skipper almost went on his knees to me – and I damn' nearly got the eldest Boyd-Leathers leg before. He was plumb in front but the Stripford umpire, a man I'd never liked, was mending his pipe at the crucial moment.

Our lot were pretty depressed, and Stripford were cock-ahoop. 195 is a lot of runs for public employees to get. I was beginning to regret my generosity. It had not been my intention to play the good loser to Hugh Boyd-Leathers' back-slapping winner. I wished I was back in my study listening to Brahms *intermezzi*. But I wasn't. I was watching our openers batting like . . . well, like ticket inspectors. When my turn came to stride to the middle our score was 29 for 4. The cause was lost. My quixotic gesture had curdled in the cup. Humiliation stared me in the face.

Up until my arrival Hugh Boyd-Leathers had been fielding at deep backward point. Now he hurried forward to silly mid-off, no more than half a dozen paces from the crease. He leered at me – actually leered. He had the look of a policeman waiting below a window as an unsuspecting burglar climbs out. I could imagine him in the clubroom bar, later, describing the situation. Something snapped inside me. Reason and discipline fled. I became that most despicable of beings – a tonker.

The bowler – Hector Ascott-Bouvier, who can be fastish – raced towards me and flung over his arm. I didn't see the ball. I whirled the bat in a great arc, felt leather on willow, and . . . there was Boyd-Leathers clutching the little red devil to his chest, shouting hysterically, and throwing it into the air. Great God in Heaven, I prayed, not out first ball! Sweet gentle Jesus, not *first* ball. Please . . .

Suddenly everybody's attention was directed to the Ingbury skipper, who was at the other end. He was pointing towards fine leg. The umpire, Major Ascott-Bouvier, father of the bowler, looked displeased. The expression of hideous pleasure began to melt from the secretary's face. The skipper was saying, '. . . you've got four men backward of square on the leg side. So that must have been a no-ball.' The umpire glared at the skipper, glared at the fieldsmen, threw his pebbles angrily to the ground and spat out the words, 'Dammit . . . no-ball. Bloody barrack-room lawyers!'

When I am finally laid to rest my nearest and dearest will wonder at the soft smile that plays around my icy lips.

'He died content,' they will say, and they'll be right because, however long the innings of my life lasts, I shall never, never forget the look of agony on Hugh Boyd-Leathers' face. I won't try to describe the expression – it would take the combined talents of Anton Chekhov and Ira Gershwin to do that. I will simply say that nothing, not the offer of a dukedom or an invitation to open for Glamorgan, could have been sweeter to me at that moment.

The rest is history.

Nothing Ascott-Bouvier, *père* or *fils*, could do was going to bother me now. My game was in the hands of the greatest Coach of them all. I hit every ball off the sweet spot and finally had nine disgruntled Stripfordians sulking on the boundary. I was dropped five times, and survived three disgracefully childish lbw appeals. My final tally was 52. We'd won by six wickets. What more is there to say? True, my partner had managed to scratch together 104 not out, but he was a spear carrier in this production, a modest walker-on.

I was never invited back to Stripford. Not one of them could look me in the face. Hugh Boyd-Leathers slunk off to Muscat and Oman shortly afterwards. He told everybody it was business, poor devil.

I've played several good innings in my time, but only one that could honestly be described as great. I wish one or two others had been there to see it; Leslie Ames, for instance, and my father, who once said that at the wicket I looked like a man trying to throw a saddle on an octopus. He, and Leslie Ames, would have enjoyed it.

2

The Unspeakable in Gloucestershire

My definition of a foreigner is someone who doesn't understand cricket. Thus Sikhs, and Queenslanders, and quite a lot of Dutchmen are not foreigners. Frenchmen, on the other hand, and Bulgarians, and most women, are. In this underprivileged group I have always included Spaniards. They're a fine race of people, accomplished at many things – stamping their feet, for example – but they are for ever excluded from Nirvana by their lack of interest in cricket.

This said, you will understand my surprise when, on flicking through some old score books, I came across the name Enrique Blanco Encalada going in at number five for Chigworth, a small cricketing community in the Forest of Dean. Foreigners, of course, are sometimes allowed to take part in matches, usually for the amusement of the spectators. Who has not seen the burly American, bat on shoulder, quite unable to cope with movement off the pitch? Or the visiting representative of the Vatican who refuses to hit the ball until it has hit him? These gutsy characters merely confirm the point: foreigners cannot play cricket. Yet Blanco Encalada, E., scored 49 not out in a total of 117, and took three catches.

Who was this improbable Iberian? The offspring of exiles, perhaps, brought up within the shadow of Kennington Oval? Or an Englishman keen to conceal his identity for reasons of national security? Or simply a Spaniard from Spain who had stumbled on, say, a copy of Halfyard's *The Only Game* and found himself bewitched by its message? Mind you, he could play a bit, too, which only deepened the mystery.

I didn't sleep well that night, and at four in the morning was drinking tea and leafing through Murchison's *Sport and the Inquisition*. But there was no suggestion of the game ever existing beyond the Pyrenees. Nor in Brownrigg's *The Armada: A Sportsman's View*. In parenthesis, may I just say that Tommy Brownrigg's book is remarkable for two pieces of original research. First, he is adamant that Drake was playing cricket when told of the approach of the enemy fleet, and had just come on at the Hoe end. His refusal to abandon the game will make sense to anyone who has ever hung about for hours in the deep waiting to get his hands on the ball. Brownrigg also points to a lamentable absence of organization aboard the Spanish ships. No deck games had been arranged. There were no quoits, no deck tennis, nothing. It was inevitable, therefore, that when the going got tough the Spaniards were in a totally non-competitive frame of mind.

Having drawn a blank in my own library I decided to cast my net wider. The gentleman at the Spanish embassy was very courteous, but unhelpful. He offered me a glass of sherry and suggested I try the United Nations. Instead I went to Chigworth. The year of Encalada's innings had been 1946, but I assumed there would still be a few villagers around who would recall those days. In the public bar of the Prone Alderman I came across several elderly gentlemen all of whom claimed to have lived their entire lives in Chigworth. Two had actually wielded the willow, but none had come across the flashing Spaniard. Yet I got the impression my enquiry had touched a nerve.

An unease, a shiftiness almost, descended on the company.

The Rector was a youngish man, a newcomer, but his study walls were lined with books of local history. I discovered, for instance, that a Chigworthian had crossed the Gulf of Bothnia in a large flower-pot, the hole stopped with a rolled-up copy of the *West Gloucestershire Advertiser*. Remarkable. Also that Chigworth duck pie had been served to George V prior to Hazel Buck's victory at Wimbledon. But there were no Spaniards, sporting or otherwise.

I showed the Rector the score book and he immediately recognized the names of several local families, but that of Blanco Encalada meant nothing. He suggested I spoke to Rufus Butt, the Sage of Chigworth, who resided under the protection of three dutiful daughters. He warned me that Butt's brain was not the finely tuned instrument of former years, but that if I was lucky enough to catch him on a lucid day he would certainly know the answer to my question.

Snapdragon Cottage would have been the ideal subject for a picture postcard but for the abandoned coal mine at the end of the garden. The door was opened by a handsome lady in her early sixties who, having checked my credentials, showed me into her father's study. This was a small, cluttered room. A log steamed sullenly in the grate and there was a strong smell of Ransley's Alpaca Mixture, a he-man blend no longer available to the general public. The smoker himself perched in a wing chair facing the fireplace. He was extraordinarily small. I doubt if he was any larger than 'Knuckles' Fleetwood, the late Flintshire wicketkeeper (who, when crouching behind the stumps, was invisible to the incoming bowler). Also, like 'Knuckles', he was incredibly old.

'Friend of the Rector's come to see you, Father,' said the daughter, as if it was no more than he deserved. 'About the cricket.'

Butt drew heavily on his pipe then turned his head in my direction. The face was like the inside of a fossilized walnut, something I've never seen but have often speculated over. Everything about it was dead, except the eyes. They glittered like emerald earrings in porridge. Carefully he took the pipe from his mouth and stared at it as if *it* had spoken, not his daughter.

'What year?' he asked the pipe.

'I was especially interested in 1946,' I said.

He glared at the reeking object in his hand, displeased by its answer. Then he snapped 'Leave us', and the daughter hurried out. For a moment he was silent, simply staring into the fire that was dying of malnutrition. Then he nodded to himself.

'I knew it would happen. It was only a question of time before some busybody would come through that door, bringing down shame on our heads.'

I stared at my minuscule host in astonishment. Busybody! Me? As you will very well know, I am shy and self-effacing to an almost pathological degree. Had Butt been a few years younger I'd have told him so in no uncertain terms. Instead, I merely observed:

'I am here simply to enquire about a Señor Blanco Encalada who once appeared for Chigworth . . .'

'I know perfectly well why you've come,' interrupted Butt. 'To drag aside the veil of decency that has concealed our humiliation all these years.'

I felt this was going too far. We and the Spanish people have not always seen eye to eye, but surely to use the word 'humiliation' about one innings in one trifling match was getting things out of proportion?

'He scored 49 runs,' I said. 'Perhaps he wasn't English but, by God, he was a cricketer!'

Butt glanced at the portable volcano in his hand. It

seemed to have come out in sympathy with the fire, and the Sage laid it aside.

'You obviously know very little about the circumstances.'

'Only what appears in the score book.'

'And if I don't satisfy your curiosity you'll go rooting about elsewhere.'

'Well . . .'

'For that reason I'm prepared to tell you the whole story – on two conditions. One, you never repeat a word of it to a living soul, and, two, I take possession of the score book.'

I agreed immediately.

The gnome of Chigworth blew his nose on a large spotted handkerchief, and began. For a Sage his narrative style left a lot to be desired, so for the benefit of modern readers I shall cut a few corners in the re-telling of the story.

Chigworth, it seems, was away to Little Pursloe, a mediocre team frequently emasculated by its neighbours. The Chigworth president was Major-General Sir Goss Wickenden, inventor of the Wickenden Infantry Pencil. Lady Wickenden and their beautiful daughter, Rowena, had spent the war in Gibraltar, where the young lady had drawn attention to herself by wrestling with the troops on the beach.

One person in particular had been struck by her clear English skin and watery blue eyes. This was Enrique, son of the distinguished Castilian double agent, Manuel Blanco Encalada. Rowena and Enrique used to meet secretly behind the submarine pens and in no time a passionate love affair was in full swing.

Soon after this the war ended, and the Wickendens returned to Gloucestershire. Sir Goss re-established the village team and civilization returned to Chigworth. But Enrique's passion burned as fiercely as ever. He, too, came to England and took a room at the Poacher's Arms, Drude.

Clandestine telephone calls were made, again Pyramus met his Thisbe, and all the air was filled with the music of Tolchard Evans.

However, sport though she was, Rowena wanted the knots of passion tied within the sight of God, who can always spot a granny. She dragged her unwilling Spaniard out of the bushes and into the paternal presence.

'Daddy,' said Rowena, 'Enrique wants to ask you something.'

The bluff old soldier regarded Blanco Encalada with distaste. Everything about him was wrong: his size, his nationality, his eating habits, the colour of his skin, the tightness of his trousers. Yet Rowena represented a growing menace to the good name of the Wickendens. Her desires, harnessed to a ruthless will, threatened to bring scandal and reporters showering down on their heads. The Major-General decided to play it canny.

'Tell you what I'll do, young feller,' he said. 'If you want to marry my daughter, you'll have to prove to me, and to Rowena's mother, that you're made of the right stuff.'

'Stuff?' muttered the baffled Iberian.

'If you can play a straight bat while all around are sweeping across the line I'll give the matter serious consideration. We're playing Little Pursloe in a couple of weeks' time. Awful team. If you're game, I'll put your name down.'

The little Spaniard left the house in shock and dismay. Straight bat? Stuff? He would happily have fought wild bulls for the right to carry Rowena off to his hacienda, but what was this Little Pursloe across the line? The lovers made their way to a private place.

'Father's a pig,' said Rowena. 'He wants to make you play cricket.'

'It is not possible,' pleaded Enrique.

'Of course it's possible,' said the girl. 'I'll coach you. I'm pretty good. You may not score a lot of runs but, by God, you'll have the straightest bat in the county.'

They practised in the nets at Drude. Village youths were hired to bowl at Enrique, in return for tubes of sherbet, while Rowena screamed at him from silly mid-off. By the end of the first week he had made no progress at all. By the following Friday, two days before the match, he'd actually gone backwards. Despair fell across them like a large black eiderdown. Enrique was for suicide, quick and honourable, but Rowena saw no percentage in this for herself, so vetoed it. There had to be another way.

When a girl like Rowena Wickenden wants something badly enough, the rules of civilized behaviour cease to exist. She devised a plan that was not only ludicrous but underhand. It had no chance at all of succeeding.

At midday on Sunday the Wickenden Lagonda failed to start. Luckily their good neighbour, Mr Hipgood, chanced to look over the hedge at the crucial moment and offered to drive Sir Goss to the match. By two-thirty they still hadn't arrived. But Rowena and Enrique, travelling independently, had. Taplin, the Vice-Captain, welcomed the Spaniard rather coolly, and told him, slowly and loudly, that he was down to bat at number five. Enrique nodded dumbly. Five or five hundred, it was all the same to him. Having received his instructions, he and the President's daughter withdrew to the far side of the field, where they settled down in the deep shade of a clump of oaks.

From the start everything went badly for Chigworth. Little Pursloe had deceitfully obtained the services of a good bowler and, not content with this, bowled him, unchanged, from the winding-house end. The Chigworth wickets fell at 2, 5 and 11. There was a plucky show of resistance from Vice-Captain Taplin, but soon he played all round a leg-cutter and was trudging back to the pavilion.

Four wickets down, but where was Blanco Encalada, E.? Ah, there, stepping shyly to the crease from the other side of the field. He was hardly an encouraging sight with his sallow complexion, sloping shoulders and over-large pads. Un-English was hardly the word for it.

He took guard, and ten Pursloe fielders edged hungrily forward. The ball was fastish, straight and rising. It missed bat, stumps and wicketkeeper. Four byes. Taplin and the rest of the Chigworthians sighed and lowered their gaze. What a day to introduce a ruddy garlic-basher into the team! But now came the sound of ball on bat and the cry of 'Y-e-e-e-s!' from Hillyard, the other batsman. The Spaniard had actually hit the ball – clean through extra cover for four! Eyes were nervously raised and breaths held. Crack! Away it went past mid-wicket for three, right off the meat.

Yes, the visitor from overseas *did* play straight while all around were dabbing and flashing and, as has been revealed, did score an undefeated 49 and take three catches. Had the curtain fallen at this point the events of that day would have sunk gently into the leaf-mould of legend, only to be remembered perhaps when rain stopped play and time hung heavy. But life was less obliging.

At the fall of the last Pursloe wicket Blanco Encalada sped off in the direction of the oak trees. His colleagues may have assumed that this was in response to his Latin modesty. If so, they assumed incorrectly. Obadiah Wilkins, the village Peeping Tom and postmaster, had been observing the final overs of the match from a hide quite near the oaks. He now witnessed a remarkable sight. In the supposed privacy of the brushwood Encalada removed his flannels, only to reveal limbs of the purest white. He then produced a rather pretty blue dress from under a bush and put it on. Familiar though he was with the bizarre, Obadiah was aghast. Now a second figure emerged from the undergrowth – unquestionably male – and set about washing the cricketer's face with a damp sponge. Away came the sallow complexion to expose the pink cheeks of a young person of the opposite sex. In less than three minutes Señor Enrique Blanco Encalada had turned into Rowena Wickenden.

That, of course, was that. Wilkins could hardly wait to tell his tale to the Little Pursloe captain, and he, numb with outrage, told Taplin. Even before the last boot was unlaced the story was common property. Chigworth had played a woman!

The rest is history. Of course Sir Goss had to resign and the name of Chigworth was crossed off every fixture list in the county. The real Blanco Encalada returned to Spain in disgrace. Rowena married a taxi driver from Rotherham and only came home at Christmas. There were one or two other things I wanted to ask the Sage as he stared glumly into his grate of ashes. For instance, did Rowena ever play again? After all, ladies with genuine talent don't grow on trees. And, I wonder, did Encalada ever understand about getting his foot to the pitch of the ball? Spaniard he may have been, but even some Danes can do it. And for how long did the cloud of shame and banishment hang over Chigworth? An entire generation, or more? I didn't ask. And now I shall never know, because I gave the Sage my word. Nothing on earth would tempt me to break that confidence. Ch*gw*rth's vile secret is safe with me.

3

A Fine, if Misunderstood, Cricketer

My cousin is a far better cricketer than I am. I say this with pride and without fear of contradiction. His talent with both bat and ball has been the subject of comment by some of the shrewdest observers of the game. The Rev. Clifford Dunchild, who has umpired more Northern Clergy *v.* Southern Clergy matches than anyone alive, besought my cousin to take the cloth because he had never seen the googly so skilfully disguised.

People sometimes ask me if I was ever jealous of my cousin. How laughable! How could one be jealous of a man who has been known to go to the wicket wearing a hook-on beard in playful imitation of the great Doctor – and still manage to squeeze the ball between first and second slip?

It's true there was another side to his character. Drink, for instance. I've known him take up a glazed stance in front of the heavy roller at eleven-thirty in the morning and ask for two legs. And he adopted the habit of taking a large metal flask with him to the wicket. This would be crammed into his trouser pocket and, if struck, would give out a sound like a tortoise falling into a saucepan. He was also a shameless liar. And a lecher. His personal habits were not exemplary, and he owed money all over the county. But once he stepped out on to the broad green stage all that was forgotten. The sheer joy of seeing a consummate artist at work made one realize how trivial other things were.

I mention my cousin because at this particular moment he is struggling to re-establish himself in society. He's had these difficult moments before, invariably being pestered by cuckolded husbands and outraged creditors. But how can one do one's best when hounded by such people? Certainly he's not perfect, but who is? Surely one can overlook a few shortcomings in a man who was once able to negotiate the sale of a gold wrist watch to first slip while driving the ball wide of mid-on.

Perhaps the greatest injustice ever done to my cousin was the three-month suspended sentence he received for his alleged part in the Knockington Hall caper. The charges brought against him were never proved, and the Georgian silver spoons found in his cricket bag later were almost certainly planted by a jealous opponent. On top of that, the magistrate who referred the case to a higher court was a close personal friend of the Hon. Lance Mortimer-Legge whose wife was often to be seen arriving late in her Bentley at matches in which my cousin was playing.

I would like to give a brief account of the Knockington Hall match for the purpose of setting the record straight, and of demonstrating to any fair-minded person that a cad is not necessarily a crook.

Knockington is in Dorset, and the Hall is set in one of those locations that appear to have been created by God for the purpose of maddening townies, Marxists and foreigners. The vast park rolls green and sweet, the trees cluster anciently, the larks clamour, and there are flowers at your feet. The breeze is always from the South, and the Hall itself is an immodest Late Tudor masterpiece.

The owner was Sir Jacklyn Dredge whose only contribution to human happiness was the creation of a cricket pitch within the grounds, the one thing the Elizabethans had forgotten to provide. (I won't accept that this was done deliberately, on the principle that perfection demands one small blemish. I think the architect had another job to go to and the cricket field went clean out of his mind.)

The pitch was used four or five times a year for matches between Sir Jacklyn's own team and, because of his contacts in the grocery business, such sides as the Bird's Custard XI or the H.P. Sauce XI. My cousin was a regular with the Sainsbury's team. He was never employed by that excellent company but is said to have had a hand in the design of the white snood worn by girls on the bacon counter.

The match in question was arranged for the third Saturday in August, a day which turned out hot and sunny (in accordance with the Agreement between God and the Proprietor). The Sainsbury's XI was strong. It included not only my cousin, but also Jan 'Fumbler' Spyke, the Orange Free State stumper, and Claude de Toqueville, the only French-Canadian ever to trouble Walter Hammond (out on the pitch, that is). Even so, Sainsbury's didn't expect to have it all their own way. The home team included several 'resting' county players, and Toombs, a local man who usually bowled very fast at the batsman's head.

Sainsbury's fielded first, and I must briefly arrest the almost irresistible momentum of the story to clear up the question of the toss. When Breakspeare, Sainsbury's captain, and Sir Jacklyn arrived in the middle it was discovered that the noble knight was without a coin. It was suggested later that my cousin had actually stolen this from Sir Jacklyn's back pocket, either for gain or for a darker purpose shortly to be revealed. I utterly reject the first. Only that morning he had borrowed a fiver from the head gardener, and was not short. It is true, however, that he had pressed an antique Cuban escudo into Breakspeare's hand a few minutes earlier, and the question has been asked, why? I don't deny that this is one of the world's few coins with a head on both sides, but one shouldn't lose sight of the fact that my cousin had a quixotic streak in him. I think it was intended as a gift, nothing more. Perhaps it was not the most obvious time or place for the giving of presents but, for Heaven's sake, we're not all pressed from the same dreary mould.

Sir Jacklyn, discovering he had no coin, accepted Breakspeare's offer of the escudo. He spun it, Breakspeare called heads, as was his custom, and for reasons already explained found he had called correctly. He then inserted the home team. Why? Obviously because the ball swings before lunch at Knockington. Some trouble-maker – it may have been the magistrate – suggested that my cousin had talked Breakspeare into it. How ludicrous! Obviously the idiot had never found himself playing down the wrong line to a ball of full length.

Be that as it may, Knockington batted and, as the record shows, ran amok. They declared in the early afternoon having scored 252, an astonishing total on a difficult wicket. My poor cousin was singled out as the villain of the piece. Certainly he dropped seven catches and had ninety-two scored off his five overs, but the greatest cricketers in history have nodded from time to time. Didn't Bradman get a duck at the Oval? Wasn't the incomparable Lindwall hit for three consecutive sixes at Trent Bridge? No? Then it must have been someone else.

My cousin was also pilloried for his wild throws at the wicket which, because of inadequate backing up, produced an additional fifty-nine runs for the opposition. I put this down to boyish enthusiasm, not malice as did the magistrate. Certainly not all the throws passed close to the stumps, even those directed from first slip, but I refuse to believe it was done deliberately. My cousin was too good a cricketer.

When the Sainsbury's openers went out it was already felt that the cause was lost. The mood of despair deepened when both of them fell to Toombs with only eleven on the board. The word 'fell' has a particular poignancy when applied to this bowler. Sainsbury's number one, a blue, collapsed across his stumps trying to fend off a murderous beamer, and Breakspeare was struck in the ribs and had to be rushed to the cottage hospital. At 21 for 5 the match, as a contest, was dead. The situation required divine intervention rather than just a simple miracle and such exalted participation is rare in cricket.

But perhaps it was a slow day in Heaven, because very soon all those present were privileged to witness a drama the like of which has never been seen before or since in the county of Dorset. My cousin dragged himself to the wicket, weighed down by the disapproval of his own team-mates, plus the flask in his pocket. It's conceivable that some of the Sainsbury's players actually hoped he'd get a duck, and maybe a couple of small bruises, as a punishment for his earlier sins, though such feelings would be repugnant to that most humane of commercial enterprises in whose colours they were playing.

At the non-striker's end was a piano tuner called Cluff who seldom scored many runs but was the very devil to get out. His judgement of line and length was impeccable, as was his rendering of 'The Merry Peasant'. My cousin paused for a quiet word with Cluff.

'When I say run, bloody run. Otherwise stand aside and keep your head down.'

Toombs, who had been rested after felling the openers, now came back for his second spell. He peered at my cousin for a moment as if selecting the exact piece of anatomy he wished to destroy. The decision taken, he walked back to his mark, turned, then raced in. The ball exploded from his hand at an inhuman speed. It sped parallel to the ground, arriving almost immediately in the vicinity of my cousin's left ear. My cousin did not step back, or sway. He raised his bat in the manner of a Furtwängler and, as if summoning an invisible orchestra to play, expelled the ball to leg. All eyes stared up into the sky. There was silence for several seconds, then the sound of tinkling glass. Another longish pause now, followed by the sight of Yardley, Sir Jacklyn's butler, approaching from the house, carrying the ball on a silver salver. He presented it to Sir Jacklyn, fielding at extra cover, and withdrew.

We were told the ball had entered the house via the pantry window, narrowly missing a VAT inspector. Later the police measured the distance from crease to window and came up with the figure of three hundred and five yards. What more can one say?

The ball was thrown back to Toombs who returned to his mark. A great darkness clouded what was, at the best of times, a sombre visage. He moved forward, two short steps first, then the long, distance-devouring strides of the enraged antelope. His arm was a blur of white, the ball a pink smudge on the air. It was directed at my cousin's left foot and, had it hit, would have buried itself, and the foot, and a large part of the leg, several feet in the ground. My cousin moved an inch or so outside the line and flicked delicately at the ball, rather like a man removing an ant from his trousers with a sprig of basil. Again all eyes swivelled skywards. This time the silence was followed by a distant splash.

The great lake at Knockington is a little nearer to the cricket pitch than is the house, but not much. It took six farm labourers twenty minutes to declare the ball lost. A new one was fetched, and that over cost Toombs twenty-five runs. My cousin took a single from the last ball and helped himself to twenty-seven from the bowler at the other end.

During the next twenty minutes or so word spread to the furthest corners of the Knockington estate. Nut-brown retainers, heavy with years and scorn, crept out of their cottages to see the crucifixion of Toombs, who wasn't particularly popular in the village. Laundry maids, second butlers, novice stable boys, and cook herself, emerged slowly from the great house and gathered at the boundary. Soon it seemed that there were about twice as many more people watching than actually lived in the neighbourhood, which is a measure of my cousin's sudden popularity.

To my eternal regret I was not of their company. I was in Buxton that day watching professionals batting like undertakers. When the stories came back I felt very much like those gentlemen in England now a-bed, accurs'd I was not there. Allow me to give a few dry statistics. My cousin hit seventeen sixes, twenty-one fours, and twice ran five. Four cricket balls were lost that day, even though everyone in the village was out looking for them. While Cluff at the other end was garnering eleven runs my cousin scored 222. The imagination of the reader will clothe these bones with the flesh of human drama; the desperation of the fielders, the intoxication of the visitors, the suicidal misery of Sir Jacklyn Dredge. The retreat from Moscow was a tiresome inconvenience compared to the agonies suffered by the Knockington XI.

Long before the end Toombs was led from the field in tears, and Sir Jacklyn developed a twitch he's never quite shaken off. The crowd grew increasingly hysterical, baying like wolves for 'more, more . . .' When the winning run had been scored the fielders dragged themselves away like wraiths. The Sainsbury's players, winners by five wickets, lifted my cousin shoulder high and bore him in triumph from the field of battle.

The scene that met their astonished gaze as they entered the house had nothing to do with cricket at all. That is my belief, and nothing, not even money, will make me change my mind, despite what so-called lawyers may say.

In brief, Knockington Hall had had visitors. While every human being over the age of three months had been absent from the house, watching my cousin and looking for lost balls, hoodlums had broken and entered, helping themselves to a van-load of Sir Jacklyn's pricier pieces. The evil-doers themselves were soon apprehended. A laneful of cows, en route for the milking shed, is a barrier impervious to even the most desperate of criminals, and the Dorset Constabulary soon had them behind bars. So far, so good. But now someone voiced the notion that my cousin had been a party to the enterprise by wilfully distracting attention away from the house.

The idea was so preposterous that . . . well, if my cousin had had any friends they would simply have roared with laughter. As it was, nobody laughed. People began to remember small, unimportant details, such as the Cuban escudo, and from those small details a mean, circumstantial case was cobbled together.

The judge hated cricket, that was quite clear. He pretended not to understand terms such as 'silly mid-off' and kept mumbling about people not having something better to do with their time.

Counsel for the Defence was totally inept. More than once he referred to my cousin as 'this young athlete on the threshold of a brilliant career', which the court was asked to relate to the heavy-gutted Falstaffian figure in the dock. The Prosecution, on the other hand, was icily efficient.

Breakspeare appeared for the Defence, but was putty in

the hands of the Prosecution. He lamely admitted that he had never known anyone perform so badly in the field, and so brilliantly at the crease. What sort of friend and captain is that? Things were looking bad.

Ironically, my cousin was rescued from a long custodial innings by the evidence of Toombs, appearing for the Prosecution. Only a batsman of incredible talent could have played him as my cousin played him, said Toombs. Only a batsman combining the talents of Sir Jack Hobbs and Sir Donald Bradman could possibly have done it. The jury was deeply impressed by the social quality of the examples given; also by the whiteness of Toombs' knuckles as he gripped the edge of the box. Here was a man who had been to the very Pit, and looked in. Here was a man to believe.

My cousin went on a longish tour of the Aleutians immediately after the case, and became the first man to score a hundred before lunch at that latitude. When he returned to England he found many pavilion doors closed to him. Even the most occasional of Rovers and Wanderers preferred to struggle rather than stain their score books with his name.

But shed no tears for my cousin. I read only last week in the *Kentish Messenger* that a cricketer, wearing a large beard and a metal thigh-pad, took 6 for 11 at Maidstone playing for the Northern Sinfonia against Barming All Stars. Perhaps it wasn't my cousin performing under an assumed name. Perhaps the beard was real and the iron thigh-pad simply that. But I noted that at the end of the report it said that a Benito Mussolini concrete gnome, missing from a nearby garden, had mysteriously turned up at the headquarters of Messrs Crosse & Blackwell. It has a familiar ring, and suggests to me that the mischievous old Beethoven of the willow is back in business. And damn'd good luck to him!

4

Tea

Passion is bad for cricketers. Like beer and anger it can play havoc with a batsman's footwork and cause fieldsmen to fumble quite easy catches. It's not even good for ladies involved with the game. It's perfectly all right for women to get ideas about actors and blast-furnace managers, but once they tangle with cricketers they have set their feet on a stony path.

The following events were narrated to me by a cycle repair mechanic from Wiltshire. I'll say no more.

Belinda Schofield was a widow, though one might not have guessed it from her appearance. She was vivacious and comely, and not at all old. She'd only very recently moved to the village – taken the Mountfords' charming old cottage down by the bridge – so she was still a bit of an unknown quantity. The Appledores called on her, and the rector, and Major Caxton, and old Mrs Villiers with a box of lettuces. The verdict after six weeks was that Mrs Schofield was a rather nice person. Clara Caxton thought she was perhaps a little older than one had at first thought, but, as Rosamund Appledore pointed out, that was perfectly natural in someone still of marriageable age.

Strictly speaking, Belinda Schofield wasn't sure she was a widow at all. Gregory had sailed out of Poole harbour one bright spring morning and had never been seen again. Several days later his small yacht was discovered smashed to bits on the Needles. The coast guards, and the police, and the man from the DHSS were in no doubt that Gregory had been struck by a squall and carried overboard. They were profoundly sympathetic.

'But, really, how very sad,' said Rosamund Appledore. 'She's such an energetic person, such a *doer*, the sort of person who needs a husband round the house simply to mop up all that surplus drive.'

They introduced her to every energy-sapping person in the village: Mrs Hancock who ran the tennis club, Mrs Wilmington who never stopped gardening, Mrs Ruff who rode to every meet for fifty miles, and Mrs Boxingford who believed in weaving your own clothes, building your own house, and, if necessary, digging your own coal. Mrs Schofield met them all and allowed herself to be drawn into their exhausting lives.

Yet deep down inside Belinda Schofield was not totally happy. Often after a hectic day she would lie awake listening to the brook pattering by in its stony bed and wonder about Gregory. Was he really dead? Was he really full fathom five, eyeless, under the secretive sea? Or had he stage-managed the whole thing in order to spend all his time with Janet Flood in Littlehampton? She'd caught them together only two weeks before his disappearance. Janet was more bosomy than Belinda. And highly plausible. After the discovery of the yacht she'd nearly rung Janet, but at the last moment hadn't. What was the point? After all, it wasn't as if she was heartbroken. Gregory was one of those men who are neither objectionable nor unobjectionable. Just bland. In fact her estimation of Janet Flood as a homewrecker and *femme fatale* had actually gone *down* because of her interest in Gregory.

Then Belinda met Hugh Wilson-Mills.

It was at a tennis party given by the Hancocks. There seemed to be hundreds of people everywhere – all over the house and the gardens and the orchard and the stables and the pub across the road. Some were still in sweaty singlets, hot from the tennis court, others in immaculate summer garb, not a hair out of place. Wilson-Mills was one of the immaculates in spotless pale-blue blazer, creaseless white shirt, knife-edged slacks and cream leather slip-on shoes. He wasn't terribly handsome, and his hawk-eyed wife was never more than a hydrangea away, but Belinda Schofield thought he was smashing.

Hugh refilled Belinda's glass with 'cup', and they chatted.

'Have you been playing tennis, Mrs Schofield?'

'Good heavens, no. Be slaughtered. Do call me Belinda.'

'Do you ride at all?'

'Not for years.'

'You must get to know Betty Ruff. She never stops riding.'

'Then I'll have to wait until she falls off.'

'Well, yes, ha-ha-ha . . .'

And so on.

They were broken up by Mrs Wilson-Mills but met again in the herb garden about half an hour later.

'Do you play badminton?'

'No,' said Belinda.

'What about a swim?'

'What, now? I haven't got my things.' And then, 'I sing.'

'You what?'

'Gilbert and Sullivan, stuff like that.'

'I don't think anyone sings round here. What about squash? Or fishing?'

'I suppose I could learn.' A note of desperation crept into Belinda's voice.

'Well, I couldn't teach you,' said Wilson-Mills. 'Can't stand all that leaping about. I enjoy my cricket, but apart from that . . .'

Cricket! A cold shiver ran down Belinda's spine. How awful! Of all the games and pastimes in the world cricket was the most sexless, the least seductive, the ultimate deterrent to intimacy. The one thing to be said in Gregory's favour was that he had had no interest in cricket.

'Yes,' continued Wilson-Mills, 'we play most Saturdays. Not a bad little team. You must come down and watch us.'

'I'd *love* to,' said Belinda.

He glanced at her.

'You don't score, do you?'

'Score?'

'You know, the runs and things. In a sort of book.'

'No, but . . . if someone showed me how . . .'

The almost blank expression on Hugh Wilson-Mills' face concealed a mixture of emotions. Scoring at cricket is not difficult; no more difficult, say, than playing the harpsichord. But showing someone how to do it can be tiresome and bad for a relationship in its early days. Really one needs to watch a competent scorer at work, someone infinitely patient, but not someone one hopes to get to know better. The trouble is the novice always wants to know why, and in cricket there's often no answer to that question. For instance:

'Why do you put funny lines against that batsman?'

'Because he's out.'

'But why funny lines? They look so Byzantine.'

'Because cricket *is* Byzantine!'

'I thought it started in Hampshire.'

Or again:

'Why is everything so detailed? I mean, who cares that Bowler X gave away three runs off the second ball of his thirteenth over? Who's ever going to want to know?'

'Bowler X, for one. And his family, particularly his grandchildren.'

'I don't believe it.'

'Then why ask!'

'I'm trying to learn how to score, aren't I!'

'Dammit, did the umpire signal a leg-bye, or did he touch it?'

'Did who touch what?'

'Don't you know the first thing about the bloody game?'

'If you're going to be abusive . . .'

Hugh Wilson-Mills wanted to avoid having this sort of conversation with Belinda Schofield because, for all he knew, Mrs Schofield might turn out to be an incredibly interesting addition to village society. One always lived in hope.

'Look,' he said, 'why don't you just come and watch? Pop down on Saturday. Meet the team. There are red squirrels in the wood behind the pavilion. Lovely spot.'

By the following Wednesday Belinda Schofield had almost forgotten about the match, and the squirrels. Mr Hardfast, a yeoman who lived in the proletarian cottages on the other side of the brook, had given it as his opinion that her thatch was on the point of total disintegration.

'When the rats start leaving the thatch, that's the time to pull and patch,' he'd said.

Rats! In her lovely cottage. She immediately opened negotiations with Mr Hardfast's brother, who happened to be a thatcher, and arranged a consultation in depth. When a figure of many thousands of pounds was mentioned for a complete re-roofing, Mrs Schofield retired to her little study to examine her accounts. She was further confused by Mr Worthgrode, Mr Hardfast's touchy neighbour, who expressed the view that Mrs Schofield's thatch had at least another ten years' work in it, to say nothing of the fact that rats didn't live in thatch, because they couldn't stand heights.

On Thursday morning Belinda's sister, Rosemary, rang from Gravesend to tell her that Norman, her husband, had suddenly inexplicably got religion and was insisting she purged her wardrobe of all her Godless gossamer underwear. Belinda was interested and offered advice. Chuck out a few old items as a gesture of goodwill, but secretly hide the best pieces away against the day Norman came back down the road from Damascus. Or she could simply divorce him, which might be quicker. Rosemary said she'd think about it.

That afternoon Hugh Wilson-Mills phoned her. Disaster had struck Saturday's fixture. Mrs Partridge, who always did tea for the matches, had been called to the bedside of an ailing aunt. Was there the slightest chance that she, Belinda, could do tea for about twenty-five people? Just egg sandwiches and a few cakes. Nothing elaborate. And of course she'd be reimbursed. Oh yes, and plenty of tea to drink. There was a big metal pot in the pavilion, and some old cups and saucers. All Belinda had to do was provide the provender itself.

He sounded so dismayed, so vulnerable and cornered, that Belinda's heart melted. Of course she would do the teas. She would do teas for a dozen cricket matches if it would help. Anything to drive the pain out of that sad, brave voice.

'You're a damned fool,' said Clara Caxton, to whom Belinda had gone for a bit of advice. 'I used to help Milly Partridge once upon a time but I simply couldn't stand the sight of decently brought up men stuffing three sandwiches into their mouths at once, plus a large slice of fruit cake. Cricket turns men into gorillas. Still, if you've said "yes" then you're stuck with it . . .'

Belinda Schofield spent most of Friday making cakes. They were good cakes because Belinda was determined to impress Hugh. On Saturday morning she made egg sandwiches, then packed everything into the car. Although the match started at two-thirty Hugh had said she needn't appear until four. However, she thought she might get there a little earlier . . . put herself about.

At twelve-thirty Hugh rang.

'Everything going all right? Marvellous. Afraid I'm not going to be able to get there myself. Wife's mother unwell. But do introduce yourself to the team. Awfully nice chaps. Terribly good of you to do all this for us. Most appreciative. Give you a call next week.'

Thud! No Hugh. Just gorillas! Bloody hell! All of a sudden the cakes, so lovingly devised, and the sandwiches, so impishly beguiling, just looked like food. Gorilla food! How utterly infuriating!

She didn't leave until quarter to four. She calculated it was a twenty-minute drive to the cricket field, which she'd noticed on previous excursions, but was damned if she was going to turn up early. As she drove passed the old windmill she regretted bringing her own teapot and matching cups and saucers. They had been included for Hugh's benefit, nobody else's. Driving over the railway line she wondered why Hugh had been required to attend on Hugh's wife's mother. Was Mrs Wilson-Mills simply taking no chances?

A few miles further on, just as she was contemplating what *she* would have done if Gregory had asked her to decimate *her* wardrobe, she arrived at the pitch. A shoddy collection of men in grubby, badly fitting whites were lounging about in the field, occasionally pursuing the ball in a bored manner. Half a dozen non-players and women, and a smattering of coarse children, occupied the area in front of the peeling pavilion. Cricket! England's principal contribution to world culture. Yuck!

She drove in through the open gate and parked as near to the pavilion as possible. One or two proles glanced idly at her. She didn't know them from Adam. They didn't appear to know her. Obviously they came from that estate place just outside the village. She looked to see if she could recognize anyone from the village proper. She couldn't. She quietly sighed.

Inside the pavilion Belinda encountered what one always encounters inside cricket pavilions – two trestle tables stolen from the army while Lord Kitchener's back was turned, several incredibly heavy benches, and an awful smell made up of generations of clammy torsos, linseed oil, unfinished pork pies, socks and glue.

Was it worth it? pondered Belinda. Even if he'd been here? Probably not. And yet . . . did life hold so many promises for her that she could afford to be put off by a few blood-stained tables? No, it didn't, she decided, and set about laying out the tea.

Almost before she'd finished, the innings came to an end and a number of red-faced men appeared at the door of the pavilion. One, obviously a leader, pushed his way to the front.

'Er . . . my name's Pugh,' he said in a semi-cultured voice. 'Er . . . I don't think we've met.'

'Belinda Schofield. How do you do?'

'I didn't realize that this was being laid on,' said Pugh.

'As Mrs Partridge couldn't come I agreed to do it for her. Just this once. Do please help yourselves.'

'Fantastic,' said Pugh, and, over his shoulder, 'Tea's been laid on, fellers. Come and get it.'

It was a good tea. As cricket teas go it probably deserved a footnote in Wisden. The red-faced cricketers went through it in about four and half minutes. Not a crumb was left. Belinda's concern for the men's physical wellbeing was tempered by the thought that word would get back to Hugh. He would be impressed. He would wonder afresh about this not unattractive lady who had arrived dazzlingly in their midst. He would call on her, casually, at tea time. The possibilities were limitless . . .

On Sunday Rosemary rang to say Norman had started lecturing the cats on sin – and could she come down for a few days, please? She arrived after tea. By Monday evening Belinda was beginning to get bored by Norman. By Tuesday evening she was getting bored by Rosemary, too. After all, there were other things in life apart from clothes and the Royal Family. She began to wonder, a bit guiltily, if Norman had been driven by Rosemary to Him who is the only shield and sure comfort of those oppressed by Princes, in whom, of course, one should not put one's trust. On top of which there had been no word from Hugh Wilson-Mills. Nothing. She had seen Mrs Wilson-Mills very briefly in the post office and was rather puzzled by her smug expression. She shouldn't have had a smug expression. She should have been a trifle cool, even hostile, but she hadn't been.

On Wednesday she saw Mrs Partridge who *was* rather cool. This could have been a reaction to the excellence of Belinda's tea, but somehow she felt it wasn't. It seemed to come from a deeper level, as if Belinda had done something rather disgraceful. This was underlined by an unmistakable off-handedness on the part of Rosamund Appledore and Clara Caxton. Even the rector didn't pause for his usual chat. Was it possible that she had overplayed her hand? Were the gentlefolk of the village actually ganging up behind Mrs Partridge because she, Belinda, had set a standard in cricketing teas that Mrs Partridge would find impossible to approach, let alone equal? Had she committed an awful social gaffe?

On Wednesday evening Norman rang to say he was getting rid of the cats because they stonily refused to mend their ways. Rosemary, alarmed, immediately packed and left. Life without the cats didn't bear thinking about.

The charming little cottage seemed empty after she'd gone. Quite illogically Belinda suddenly felt passed over and left behind. Gregory was probably having a wonderful time in Littlehampton, and Rosemary would soon be enjoying a spirited defence of the cats' sexual rights. Even the ladies of the village would be having fun 'tut-tutting' at whatever it was Belinda had done.

It wasn't until late on Thursday afternoon that the tide began to turn. A knock at the door announced the arrival of someone with a faintly familiar face.

'Ah, marvellous!' declared the faintly familiar face. 'I've had a hell of a time finding you.'

'I beg your pardon?' said Belinda, edging back a little.

'We didn't know your name, that was the trouble.'

It was the semi-cultured voice that did it.

'You're . . . Mr Pugh!'

' 'Course I am.'

'But I don't understand,' said Belinda. 'Everyone in the village knows where I live.'

'In this village, yes. But I don't live here. I had to ask all around.'

'But you play for the village team.'

'Not this village team, I don't.'

'You mean, you were playing *against* this village?'

'No, this lot weren't involved at all. Their ground's up behind the church. Our ground's . . . well, you know where our ground is.'

Twenty-two unfamiliar faces. Twenty-two blank expressions. Belinda stared at Mr Pugh.

'For Pete's sake, why didn't you tell me?'

'Tell you what? Each team thought you belonged to the other team. Anyhow,' said Pugh, 'we had a whip round and collected four pounds, eleven pence, which we would like you to accept . . . '

For several hours after Mr Pugh had left Belinda sat quietly in the garden contemplating the inscrutability of life. Not that that solved any of the problems. Should she go cap in hand to Hugh and the ladies admitting her small error? Or should she pretend she'd been struck by a rare form of malaria? Should she ring Janet Flood? What about the thatch? And Norman? Oh, God . . . .

5

The Wedding of Nigel Grint

It was never the intention of cricket's founding fathers to challenge the institutions of established religion. Far from it. Personally, I would say that cricket and the supernatural form an obvious partnership. Cricket has learned a lot about self-discipline, playing with a straight bat, etc. from religion, while the church has profitably borrowed the idea of rewards in the life to come – that is to say, drinks after stumps – from cricket. Consider, for example, how many rural deans have graced the middle order across the centuries and, contrariwise, the regiments of crisp openers who have carried the Word into such places as Lake Nyanza, and Swansea. It is only when human weakness and carnal desire are introduced that the easy relationship is disturbed. The point is illustrated by the events surrounding the wedding of Nigel Grint, a chap from Leamington. I never knew Grint personally but I used to arm-wrestle with his brother, Jack, who told me the whole sorry tale.

Nigel Grint played for Spoonfield, a village in Oxfordshire. He was a seam-up bowler and a useful man in the deep. He was fairly useless with the bat and seldom went in higher than ten or eleven. But the great thing in his favour was that he cared like mad. Each Friday evening as he alighted from the London train all thought of life insurance, or whatever it was, faded from his mind to be replaced by visions of cartwheeling stumps and celebrations in the Duck and Flag.

However, the smooth surface of Nigel Grint's life was disturbed by the pebble of sexual passion. He fell in love with a girl from St Albans, Miranda Hughes, and so uncontrollable was his delight in her that marriage was proposed. The idea was tabled in the early Spring, and a date for the tying of knots fixed for the second Saturday in July. Fixed, that is to say, by Miranda and her parents. The date had some sort of arcane significance for Mother Hughes, and Miranda didn't want to get into a filthy row about it.

When Grint was told, he turned pale with shock. The second Saturday in July was the Thrugham match. All matches are important but some have a sort of mystical quality about them. The Thrugham fixture was such a one. Many, many years ago – some say as far back as 1978 – the proprietor of the Duck and Flag, eager to stimulate business, had donated a very small silver cup, to be played for annually by Spoonfield and nearby Thrugham. The visitors had won that match and carried off the trophy. The following year Spoonfield won. When they approached the proprietor of the Bounding Plough, the Thrugham hostelry, they were told that the cup had been lost, or stolen, he wasn't sure which, despite the fact that the object itself was on public display behind the bar. The proprietor claimed that that was a different cup; very similar but different.

Nothing the Spoonfield people could do had any effect on the burglars of Thrugham. Threats of legal action, boycott, arson, grassing to the police about late drinking, all fell on deaf ears. The following year the fixture was cancelled, which wasn't what mine host at the Duck and Flag had had in mind at all. 'Play 'em, and be damned!' he exhorted. 'Show 'em you don't care,' meaning *he* did, profoundly. An extraordinary meeting of the team was called and it was agreed that a succession of crippling defeats might cause the Thrughamites to regret their cupidity.

From that day forward the fixture was special. The result didn't always happen as planned, but every victory had the same sacred significance as did those of the Crusaders recapturing some treasured corner of the Holy Land. For this reason the second Saturday in July was sacrosanct.

Nigel Grint clipped his beloved in his arms and whispered mellifluously in her ear, 'I'll marry you, my darling, any time, anywhere, except on the second Saturday in July.' Miranda conveyed the message back to HQ. Mother Hughes said, 'In my family the girls have always been married on the second Saturday in July, right back as far as 1967. Tradition's important to us. That's the day you get married or not at all!'

Miranda felt uneasy. Mother Hughes, the Wazeer and Chief Executioner of 72 Brickiln Villas, St Albans, had an undinted record when it came to differences of opinion.

'Why is he being so unreasonable?' she demanded. 'Is this what your married life is going to be like, backing down and giving way all the time?'

'He has a prior engagement,' said Miranda.

'More important than his wedding!'

'Yes,' said Miranda.

Nigel didn't like the sound of it either. If Mother Hughes broke off negotiations the soft-skinned Miranda might be permanently eradicated from his life and handed on a plate to his rival, the hated Walter Woodcast, also of St Albans. Nigel wasn't sure whether it was his possible loss, or Walter's possible gain, that troubled him most. Either way, something had to be done. A summit conference was called at Brickiln Villas. Father Hughes absented himself on the grounds that whatever he said he would be treated with contempt, and Miranda kept demurely to her room.

The conference lasted two hours twenty-five minutes, and resulted in a most interesting compromise. Nigel and Miranda *would* be married on the second Saturday in July, but not at St Mildred's, just around the corner from the Villas. The ceremony would take place at St Woden's, Spoonfield, at eleven o'clock. The reception would be in the back room of the Duck and Flag, after which Nigel would join his team mates in the contest with Thrugham. Father Hughes approved the decision (not that anyone cared), but Miranda was less sure. Somehow she was becoming a minor figure at her own wedding. Had she known how it was going to turn out she might well have chucked in her hand then and there and stumped off round to the hated Walter.

One bright spot was the Rev. Plumpstead, the rector of Spoonfield. He was a loud, jovial man who believed that life was to be enjoyed. He adored his work. He thought all his duties were terrific fun, with funerals ranking only a few points behind weddings and christenings. He took an almost embarrassing pleasure in instructing Nigel and Miranda in the responsibilities of married life, and both were agog to see if he would be able to get through the actual ceremony without collapsing with laughter.

The second Saturday in July opened with a flood of sunshine, like a piece of early Delius. Miranda was disappointed. She'd hoped it would rain, thus restoring her and the wedding to centre stage. But the doves and the swallows swooped around the church as if under contract to Walt Disney and the forecast was for unbroken blue skies.

Nigel slipped off early for a clandestine look at the wicket. It was dry, with definite cracks on a length at the church end. Later it would turn. Better to bat first, he thought. But Dick Brainfarm, the skipper, wouldn't hear of it. 'If we bat first you'll have to bowl and field right up to the end,' he said. 'But if we bat second you might be able to get away early . . . you know, wedding night, and all that.'

At ten o'clock Nigel changed out of his whites and into his morning greys. The best man, Luscombe, gathered him up, drove him to the church and, together, they had a last gaze across the disordered meadows of bachelorhood before entering the beautiful stone edifice of marriage. But as they turned and walked towards the South Door an odd sight took their attention. An elderly lady on a bicycle was speeding down the village street, waving her hat in the air.

'It's all off!' she screamed at the top of her voice.

Nigel's heart missed a beat.

'What's happened?' he cried, hurrying to the gate where the elderly lady was skidding to a halt. 'What's the matter with them?'

'Beri-beri,' answered the breathless lady.

'What, the whole team?' demanded Nigel.

'The Rector,' gasped the lady. 'He picked it up in Zululand. Gets terrible bouts. Can't leave his bed.'

The Rector!

He and Luscombe looked at each other, then Luscombe hurried off to where the bride's party was gathered in a tight-lipped knot around the Wazeer.

'The Rector's got beri-beri,' he said. 'He's terribly sorry and all that . . .'

Mother Hughes looked at him as if he'd suddenly removed all his clothing. But only for a moment. Cool as a knife, she delivered her decision.

'Get another one, immediately.' She snapped her fingers impatiently. 'Arrange it at once. Anyone with the necessary qualifications. I want him here, cassocked and surpliced, in the next twenty minutes.'

Best man Luscombe and the lady on the bicycle hurried

to the Duck and Flag where there was a telephone. From memory she was able to produce a long list of possible candidates. Luscombe did the phoning and struck lucky at the third attempt. The Rev. Handiside of Little Yoppley had absolutely nothing to do and would be delighted to rush to St Woden's immediately. A message was sent to Father Hughes and Miranda in their secret hideout to delay their appearance at church until further notice. Everybody then withdrew to the back room of the Duck and Flag, where they steadied their nerves with sherry.

The only absentee was Nigel Grint. He was standing at the edge of the churchyard, hands in pockets, gazing out at the adjoining cricket field. If the ball *did* get up from a length, he mused, he'd need someone at silly point. Also someone at short third man, in case it didn't get up from a length. But who? And taken from where? He'd need three men on the leg side at the very least because of the natural slope of the ground. Damn'd tricky . . .

After quite a long time Nigel looked at his watch. It was eleven twenty-five. He wandered back to the pub where he found that the party had divided into two distinct schools. One, headed by Mother Hughes, was becoming tense and slightly hysterical. The other, headed by the best man, was becoming intoxicated. Twice Father Hughes had rung from the hideout to check that he and Miranda hadn't been overlooked in the confusion, and had been reassured with difficulty. At quarter to twelve Luscombe was persuaded to ring Little Yoppley to confirm that Mr Handiside had left. Yes, said the lady who answered the phone, he'd left within minutes of being summoned, but he was a very slow driver. Luscombe examined the map. It was about eight miles from Little Yoppley to Spoonfield. Yes, an average of less than eight miles per hour was very slow . . .

Soon after twelve the first of the Thrugham players arrived at the pub. Predictably they found the presence of a wedding party a suitable occasion to display their tastelessness. Two of them gate-crashed the back room and were ejected with incredible speed by Mother Hughes. As she slammed the door behind them she glared. She was not used to her plans going wrong. She had no experience of presiding over fiascos. She was not enjoying herself.

It was suggested that someone should go to Little Yoppley to check that Mr Handiside wasn't lying in a ditch somewhere along the way. The lady on the bicycle offered to go, but this was vetoed on the grounds that if the vicar *was* lying in a ditch the lady might have trouble getting him on to her crossbar. A member of the groom's party agreed to go, and everyone else got back to the serious business of settling their nerves.

At twenty-five past twelve the man returned with the now highly agitated Mrs Handiside. Her husband had left *hours* ago! Why wasn't he here? What had become of him? He was a very careful driver, she assured everybody, but other road users were less considerate. The best man phoned the Nabtonbury police who found it difficult to understand what the problem was, and, when they did understand, found it difficult to work up much interest. The desk sergeant promised to make a note of the information received on the appropriate form.

Dick Brainfarm, the Spoonfield skipper, arrived at about a quarter to one. He quite reasonably assumed from the condition of most of the guests that the wedding was safely over, and was shocked to learn that this was not the case as the vicar, or vicars, was/were indisposed and/or lost.

Mother Hughes, who had been lying down for a while, now re-emerged.

'Where's that woman on a bicycle?' she demanded. 'We must find another vicar immediately. I have no faith in the one that is lost and I refuse to leave this place until my daughter is married. A replacement is required. At once!'

The lady on the bicycle couldn't be found. Someone suggested going through Yellow Pages but this turned out to be a dead end. Mother Hughes cornered Mrs Handiside and insisted that she reveal the names of her husband's co-practitioners. But, as the red-eyed Mrs Handiside pointed out, they'd only been in the district three weeks and didn't know anybody. She knew lots of people in Middlesbrough, where they'd been before, but realized that would hardly be much help.

'What about your bishop?' snapped Mother Hughes.

'Bishops have to be booked weeks in advance,' sobbed Mrs Handiside. 'Anyhow, I can't remember his name. Please, all I want is my husband back . . .'

At ten past one her prayer was partially answered. The Rev. Handiside phoned to say that he was at the village of Spinfield. He had almost at once discovered his foolish mistake and was even now on his way to Spoonfield. Spinfield, it seemed, was thirty-five miles on the other side of Little Yoppley. Luscombe did a quick calculation. Thirty-five, plus eight, equalled forty-three. At a steady thirty miles an hour the journey would be accomplished in about one and a half hours, thus the wedding of Nigel and Miranda could take place at two forty-five.

Nigel hurried to find Dick Brainfarm.

'We'll have to bat first,' he said. 'We should be through the wedding and the reception by three-thirty, so I can be changed and padded up by three forty-five. And anyhow, the rough patch should be more useful after tea.'

At twenty-five past two, just as the wedding party was brushing itself down and straightening itself up in preparation for the ceremony, the two skippers wandered out to the middle. Brainfarm tossed. The Thrugham skipper called heads, and heads it was.

'We'll bat,' he said.

'Oh, lor',' said Brainfarm. 'Actually, we've got a small problem,' and explained the small problem to his opposite number. The opposite number was unmoved.

'That's your problem, brother. You should never try and mix business and pleasure. Any how, we're batting, and that's that!'

A written message was rushed surreptitiously to Nigel, now enpewed within the church. It read, 'They're batting first. Need you first change from the road end. Be as quick as you can, there's a good chap. R.B.'

Nigel looked at his watch. Two thirty-five. The church, pretty full now, was speechless with expectation. Any moment the organ would bulge into life, the vicar would appear and the whole carnival would be on the road. He would be as quick as he could but, apart from gabbling his bit, there wasn't much he could do to gee it on.

At two forty-two a small boy entered the church and slunk up to the best man. All eyes were on him as he whispered something into the best man's ear, then slunk out. Luscombe, not one hundred per cent sober, rose to his feet, turned and addressed the congregation.

'Mrs Hughes, ladies and gentlemen. I have just received a message from the Nabtonbury police. It seems that the Rev. Handiside has been apprehended by a patrol car and taken, under escort, to the police station. The charge is, driving without due care and attention and exceeding the speed limit. The police regret any inconvenience and hope that Mr Handiside will be with us a little later.'

There was a howl of hysterical laughter from the back of the church and Mrs Handiside was led out. The rest of the congregation broke into subdued muttering and gathered, like beggars, around the Wazeer. Mother Hughes' eyes glinted like frosty glass.

'Nobody leaves!' she announced in a voice that set the ancient stained glass flinching in its leaded lights. 'Nobody sets foot outside this building until my daughter and that person, there, are united in holy matrimony.'

Nigel Grint stepped forward.

'I'm sorry, Mother . . .' – he judged that the moment had arrived to use this telling form of address – '. . . I'm sorry, but we did agree on what was going to happen today. Part One: I, and Miranda of course, were to be married. Part Two: I was going to play cricket. As Part One is unavoidably delayed, I intend moving on to Part Two. If and when his reverence is released from custody and arrives on the premises perhaps you would be kind enough to let me know.'

His exit from the church was dignified yet firm. By the time Mother Hughes had filled her lungs, opened her mouth and delivered the words, 'Well, *really*, Nigel . . .!' Nigel was already halfway across the churchyard. Within minutes he had changed out of his greys and back into his whites, and was directing all his attention towards the rough patch, on a length, at the church end.

The Thrugham batsmen seemed stimulated by the presence of smartly dressed strangers all over the place. They played with fire and style and by tea had amassed 204, all out. Nigel Grint had taken 3 for 33, which was admirable considering all the distraction, but the Spoonfield team knew they had a long, hard furrow to plough.

Luscombe, who had sneaked out via the vestry, informed Grint that the police were just clearing up the business of Luscombe's first telephone call concerning the then lost Mr Handiside. They were just double checking that Handiside wasn't wanted for something, other than the wedding at St Woden's. As soon as that was all cleared up Handiside would be delivered back to Spoonfield.

Brainfarm said to Grint, 'You'd better bat early, then when the vicar turns up you can get married.'

'That's madness,' said Grint. 'We're going to have one hell of a job getting that score, without dickering with the batting order.'

'Only trying to help,' said Brainfarm.

At half-past four the Spoonfield innings opened, and a brave sight it was. Numbers one and two, equally inspired by the unusual goings-on, laid about them like lumberjacks on piece work. Such a display of controlled violence hadn't been seen in the village since Farmer Halfberry's bull, Clive, had destroyed the postman's bicycle, and that was many years ago. At 59 for 0, off twelve overs, it was looking good for the home side. But Thrugham still had a key card to play.

However, before describing the key card another, crucial, event must be related. After being escorted from the church Mrs Handiside had been steadied with sherry in the back room of the Duck and Flag. Now, coincident with the beginning of the Spoonfield innings, she felt the need for air. After wandering about for some time she found herself in the cricket field, near the long-on boundary. For a while she stood and gazed mournfully at the players. How free and gay they were, how careless of their liberty, unlike her own dear Melvyn. She was about to turn away when her attention was caught by the fielder nearest to her. It looked so like . . . Could it be . . ?

'Fabian,' she called nervously. 'Is it you?'

The fielder turned. He gazed at her in amazement, then, with a cry of delight, ran forward and gripped her hands.

'Melissa! But what on earth are you doing here?'

'What on earth are *you* doing here!'

This rather empty dialogue went on for some moments

before they came to the interesting bit, which, for the sake of brevity, is best reduced to its essentials. The fielder, Fabian, was none other than the Rev. Fabian Smallwood, only recently inducted into the living of St Crispin's, Thrugham. He was also a very old friend of the Handisides. He was *also* a cracking good cricketer.

Melissa Handiside blurted out the awful predicament in which she and the Rev. Handiside found themselves, to say nothing of the wedding party cowering in the church.

'My dear girl, I must come at once,' declared Smallwood. 'I'll just fix it with the skipper.'

Fixing it with the skipper was not the easiest job he'd had that week. The reason for this was that he, Fabian Smallwood, was the key card that Thrugham were about to play. The vicar was an off-spinner of some ability. The Thrugham committee had only discovered this very recently, but, having done so, had enjoyed a series of unlikely victories. Only the previous Saturday Smallwood had taken 5 for 14, thus helping his side to crucify the Midlands Electricity Board.

The conversation between skipper and key card was brief. Brainfarm was called in and it was agreed between them that the match would be suspended for twenty minutes while the key card joined the happy couple in marriage. Everybody left the field. Smallwood and Grint hurried to the church, the rest to the back room of the pub. Father Hughes and Miranda were instructed to appear instantly and almost before the first illicit pint had been drawn at the Duck and Flag Mendelssohn's merry march was peeling out across the countryside.

It was the first wedding ever at St Woden's where the vicar and the groom wore white and the bride appeared in dark slacks and cardigan. Everybody wept, except Mother Hughes, who was planning a national campaign to make the playing of cricket punishable by death in England as it had been under Edward III. Also it was one of the fastest weddings ever. Everything that could be decently omitted was omitted, and everything else ruthlessly edited or taken *molto allegro*. That is not to say a proper sense of solemnity was absent. Not at all. If anything the pace of the service helped to concentrate the minds of all present on the drama of the occasion. For instance, would the organist and the congregation finish the hymn together? Would the vicar absentmindedly exclude the 'I wills'? Would there be a maddening hold-up in the vestry? Would the photographer know who had married whom?

It says a lot for British common sense and guts that only nineteen minutes and twenty-seven seconds' playing time was lost. One can imagine what would have happened if this had been Italy, not Oxfordshire. The number of overs would have been slashed and the match reduced to a farce. But that didn't happen. The game was played to an exciting conclusion, Thrugham coming out winners by 11 runs. Smallwood took 4 for 29, and Grint, going in last, hit a plucky 14.

Afterwards there was a small party in the back room of the Duck and Flag where all earlier misunderstandings were laughed away and forgotten. Father Hughes danced the tango with the Thrugham wicketkeeper, and the lady on the bicycle did conjuring tricks. There was only one note in a minor key the whole evening. At ten-fifteen they received a phone call from Spanningfield in Shropshire. It was the Rev. Handiside wanting to know if two-thirty, Sunday, would be convenient for the wedding. This provoked a few smiles, but it should be remembered that without people like the Rev. Handiside the rest of us would look ordinary indeed. He may never have scored fifty nor taken three catches in an innings, but I'd bet my life that long after all the other players had left the field because of rain Handiside, M., would still be standing loyally at deep third man, waiting to be needed. And *that's* what cricket is all about.

6

The Selector

Friendships spring up between cricketers just as they do between chaps who meet in the trenches. Lifelong relationships are formed between men who might think they have nothing in common, until the day they are allocated adjoining pegs in the dressing-room. I knew a double-glazing salesman who became emotionally enmeshed with an oboist from the Hallé for no better reason than that they spent the whole of a long summer afternoon at first and second slip. Later, so I heard, they abandoned their families and went native in Dymchurch. Locals would spy them crouching side by side on the sea shore, finger tip to finger tip, waiting for the thin edge that never came.

But friendships, even cricket friendships, are not always what they seem. Just occasionally the warm smile and the reassuring grip of the forearm may hide the scheming heart of a viper. Such was the case with Captain Easington, the Hon. Sec. of a little Kentish village team. The full story was told to me over a pot of tea at Simpson's in Piccadilly by an acquaintance whom I shall refer to as O.Q., to conceal the identity of a man well-known in Intelligence circles.

Shortly after the war a group of gentlemen got together to resuscitate cricket in the charming Wealden village of Clufton-by-Audley. The club had not become entirely moribund during the years of conflict. A team of whipper-snappers, reserved occupationists and cripples had more or less kept things going while their betters were in khaki, but only just. During hostilities the pitch had developed uneven bounce, and a pair of tree pipits were nesting in the scorer's box, which suggested the lack of a proper organizing hand on the committee. Also, the wreck of a fairly large Heinkel still disfigured the boundary at long-on, forming a hazard to anyone running round from mid-wicket to take a catch.

O.Q. lived in the adjoining village of Little Audley but, because of a distinguished record with the 'I' Corps in Bexhill, he had been invited to join the team. He found the place buzzing with activity. New gear had been purchased, the pavilion repainted, and a family of badgers turfed out of the heavy roller where they'd clearly been in residence since Dunkirk. No wonder the ball sometimes kept low at the village end!

The club was in the charge of three men. Colonel Blackett lived at the Manor, so had automatically assumed the arduous role of Hon. President; Captain Easington, who owned a typewriter, was the Hon. Secretary; and Captain Hopper-White, Hon. Treasurer. Hopper-White was also captain of the team. These three comprised the selection committee, too. Thus nothing came or went within the confines of the sacred field unless approved by this Inner Secretariat. It was feudal but it seemed to work, and Clufton looked set for a bright future.

Apart from O.Q. the team was made up of local gentlemen, two farmers, one war correspondent, and a number of retired arms manufacturers. One of the gentlemen was Lieutenant Winslow, who had had one hell of a war in Delhi with the Signals. As it happened, none of the others cared much for Winslow. His flannels were post-war 'utility'; terribly white and cottony. And he wasn't exactly a monster performer. He bowled a bit and made a few runs down at seven or eight, but he wasn't the sort of player one would have missed. Yet, on Wednesday evenings when the Central Committee met to pick the team Winslow's name was never omitted from the list.

His patron, so to speak, was Captain Easington. If Blackett or Hopper-White suggested dropping Winslow and playing some young hopeful from the village Easington would 'tut-tut' and shake his head gravely.

'Not really on,' he'd say. 'I'm all in favour of bringing in new blood, but not at the expense of a chap who had such a beastly war.' Or, 'Young Wagfield deserves a game, no doubt about it, but where was *he* between '39 and '45?' (This, despite the fact that Wagfield was only eleven when war was declared.) Or again, if heavily pressed, 'I know Winslow's a bit of a twerp but, for God's sake, he was a commissioned officer. If we start picking the team simply to win matches where will it all end? Before we know where we are we'll be selecting chaps on merit! Surely there's more to cricket than that.'

It was an impenetrable argument. If cricketing ability was to be a factor in the selection of the team then where would Blackett and Hopper-White be? Blackett was an opener, and an extremely slow one. He was so defence-minded that, when he was facing, fielders would produce small books from under their shirts. The captain, Hopper-White, claimed to be an all-rounder, which in his case meant that he felt no obligation to be competent in any particular department of the game.

Easington was in a good position to make these comments. He himself never played. Apparently he'd eaten something that didn't agree with him during the siege of Tobruk and his timing had gone to bits. The rest of the team assumed that, for this reason, the Hon. Sec. had projected his deeper cricketing self on to the young Winslow. Hence the patronage. It was Easington out there, slashing and missing, dropping dollies, and being hit for consecutive fours. It was Winslow's flesh, but the invisible player at his elbow was Easington himself.

The notion was fuelled by Easington's regular and prolonged absences from the committee bench in front of the pavilion. Sometimes he never came back at all. Close friend and patron he may have been, but even *he* couldn't bear to watch his surrogate performing for more than a few minutes at a time.

It was an odd situation and, if truth be told, not one calculated to raise confidence and win matches. But the other members of the Secretariat were loyal. If the Hon. Sec. wanted his protégé to play, then play he did. Naturally there were moments of crisis. Winslow went five matches without scoring, which led to murmurings in the shower. And then the terrible day when he dropped three sitters off Hopper-White, who needed the wickets. The captain's comments were pointed, not to say hurtful. Alarmed, Easington took his friend to a distinguished old professional in Maidstone to be instructed in the rudiments of the game. The following week Winslow scored nine. Easington didn't see it because he'd gone on one of his rambles, no doubt unable to endure the tension. Such was the strength of feeling between them.

At this point in the narrative O.Q. suddenly ate all the little pieces of lemon that had been supplied with the tea. It's something you don't often see at Simpson's. I knew immediately that the man was in the grip of a deep emotion. What, I wondered, had happened all those years ago in far-off Clufton-by-Audley that had left such a mark on my friend?

In such a delicate situation it was obviously only a matter of time before crass Fate came blundering onto the scene. It chose the worst possible occasion; the match with Bashford Drifters, a team of conceited young popinjays from Tunbridge Wells.

The Drifters batted first, but only managed 92. This was because half a dozen of them had arrived early and spent overlong in the Craven Pullet. Ale may be jolly nice, *is* jolly nice, but it slows your reactions, particularly when your opponents have murder in their hearts.

At tea Blackett and Hopper-White were a-tremble with expectation. Victory seemed within their grasp. The popinjays were about to have their ears boxed and be sent scampering home to their mummies.

But the Clufton innings started badly. Blackett was still only halfway through a forward defensive prod as the stumps, bails and ball went flying past the wicketkeeper like a deckchair fired from a gun. Numbers two, three and four – the cream of the batting – played like Albanian goatherds. Only Hopper-White rose to the occasion. He swung, he drove, he swept, often hitting the ball, and the score tottered from 18 for 4 to 89 for 9.

The last batsman to join the captain was Lieutenant Winslow. This was late in the order for a man who had been coached by an ex-England player, albeit for only half an hour, but Blackett and Hopper-White were adamant. In a match as important as this Winslow would *not* bowl, *would* field as far away from the wicket as possible, and *would* bat last, there being no lower position available. Easington accepted this with his usual charm. As long as Winslow played, it didn't matter where he batted.

So . . . Three runs needed for a tie, four for a win. Surely Winslow could manage that? The captain would take the bowling. All Winslow had to do was run when he was told to run. Surely a man who had received instruction from a Test player could do that? But cricket, like love and book-binding, is impervious to logic. On that broad green stage the actors often give performances that have nothing whatsoever to do with the script.

Hopper-White was facing. Tension was at snapping point. The spectators laid aside their newspapers. Even the scorers watched. The bowler raced to the wicket and, because of the inhuman pressure on him, delivered a long-hop outside the off-stump. Hopper-White's eyes blazed. He thrashed down on it like a man mending a fence. The ball flew off his elbow and sped past point.

'Y-e-e-e-e-s!!'

Lieutenant Winslow started from his blocks like a stung horse. He completed his run while Hopper-White was still only halfway down the pitch. Winslow turned. He arrived at his own end no more than a yard behind his captain. They turned together and, side by side, ran to the striker's end, Hopper-White on his second run, Winslow on his third.

Ignorant people say that cricket is a slow game. In fact, not only is it the fastest game ever invented, it is fast in lots of different places at once, which puts it beyond popular comprehension. For instance, at this particular moment the following incidents were all taking place at the same time:

1) Cover point, who was fat but well-connected, was galloping round to stop the ball reaching the boundary.

2) The wicketkeeper was leaping from foot to foot, shouting 'Hard in – they're running two!'

3) The bowler was leaping from foot to foot behind *his* stumps shouting, 'This end, this end!'

4) Both umpires were dodging feverishly about in order (a) to see if the ball crossed the boundary, (b) to see if the batsmen were in their ground, and (c) to avoid being killed

by the ball when, and if, it was thrown in.

5) Hopper-White and Winslow, who had both now arrived at Hopper-White's end in a cloud of dust, were having a conversation that went roughly as follows:

Hopper-White: 'Get back, you foul man!'

Winslow: 'Three for a tie, sir. Chop, chop!'

Hopper-White: 'I hate you, Winslow! How I hate you!' (This last prompted by the sight of the bowler collecting the ball and breaking Winslow's wicket.)

What other game could provide so much entertainment in so many different places at once – all within a time span of some seven seconds?

What happened next was scarcely cricket. Hopper-White, magenta with rage, dragged off one soggy batting glove and hurled it at Winslow.

'You unspeakable twit!' he bellowed. 'You've run yourself out and lost us the bloody match!'

Stung by this, Winslow drew himself up to his full height.

'Now, look here,' he said. 'You were the chap they ran out, not me. I was going like a train.'

Hopper-White dragged off the other soggy glove, threw it on the ground and jumped on it.

'I shall never, ever play cricket with you again!' he shouted. 'In fact, I may never don flannels from this day forward, because they will remind me of YOU!'

'If there's one thing I can't stand,' rejoined Winslow, 'it's a bad loser!'

By this time everyone had left the field except the two batsmen. The popinjays were already in their dressing-room, tugging off their boots, laughing and telling each other what huge fun it had all been, thrashing the old 'uns. From the pavilions steps Colonel Blackett watched as Hopper-White aimed a blow at Winslow with his bat.

Winslow neatly parried it with his own bat, and counter-thrust. Hopper-White brushed this aside, and caught Winslow a telling blow on the ankle.

'You beast!' screamed Winslow. 'You absolute beast!'

With that, he unbuckled his pads, strode from the pitch, mounted his bicycle, and pedalled off in the direction of Little Willows, his house at the far end of the village.

He was in tears – tears of rage, pain and humiliation – as he kicked open his front door and stormed into the sitting-room. Two people were sitting on the sofa, Mrs Winslow and Captain Easington. Mrs Winslow's dress was a little above her knee. Easington's hand was in mid-air. Their expressions were like those of rabbits caught in headlights.

'Hopper-White is an absolute animal!' cried Winslow. 'I've just given the best years of my life trying to rid the world of people like that, and now I'm asked to partner him at the wicket! He's nothing but a bully and a beast. I shall never turn out for Clufton again. Never!'

He spun on his heel, removing a lump of carpet with his spikes as he did so, and marched to the door. His hand was halfway to the door knob when he stopped, then slowly looked back at the couple on the sofa. Mrs Winslow's fingers had crept to the hem of her skirt and were on the point of restoring a modicum of respectability to her appearance. Easington's hand was on its way back to its owner.

'I say,' began Winslow, 'you do believe me, don't you? It really was his fault. If he'd bucked up a bit he could have made the third run. But then . . . that's not the point, is it?'

From the look on their faces it was plain that Mrs Winslow and Easington also thought it was not the point.

'It was saying those awful things about me – out loud. In front of strangers. I mean, dammit, it's only a game!'

O.Q. gazed across the tea-room, the half-drunk Earl Grey now stone-cold in his cup.

There were things I wanted to know. Did Winslow stick to his vow and never play for Clufton again? What was said at the next meeting of the Central Committee? Did Blackett ever sort out his forward defensive prod? Yet I knew that wasn't the moment. O.Q., who has seen and done some pretty rum things in his time, was locked away in a private world of his own.

Then he turned and gave me a gruff little smile.

'I suppose you want to know how it all turned out. Well . . . I married her.'

'You *what*?'

'Grizelda. Mrs Winslow as was. After that last outburst Winslow packed a rucksack, jumped on his Rudge Roadster and pedalled off to God knows where, poor devil. Easington went into the Church, and I sort of lost touch with him. Which left me and . . . Grizelda. Fate does sometimes bowl you a long-hop outside the leg stump. She's an absolutely topping girl.'

He grinned boyishly.

'I say, do you think they've got any more of those lemons?'

7

'Quiet please, everybody!'

One of the least attractive expressions in the English language is 'I told you so!' It's a phrase I never use myself, unless maddened. I can't stand people who are wise both before and after the event. If my advice is ignored and disaster follows, I do not rush to the scene of the accident, waving my arms in the air. I keep away. I say nothing. But with some people it isn't easy.

Take Dudley Hewitson, for example. Not a bad chap, but wilful. Even pig-headed sometimes. I met him by chance at the Prussian Water Colours exhibition. I thought he looked harassed, and said so.

'It's my committee,' he said. 'They do go on so.'

'Committee?'

'The cricket club. We've been approached by Viking Television. They want to do some filming at Trodds.'

Trodds is the Hewitson home situated in the Lincolnshire village of Hilton Cupid. The house itself is a boring Victorian erection, late rural High Anglican, but the grounds are extensive and include the village cricket pitch.

'Well, it's your house,' I said. 'What's it got to do with the committee?'

'They want to film a cricket match,' said Hewitson. 'Not a proper game, of course. Just a few bits for some television play.'

I immediately visualized the scene. The cricket pitch, the village players standing in small groups doing nothing while some latter-day Cecil B. de Mille strides around pointing at people and making idiotic remarks like 'Hair in the gate' and 'I thought you did it so much better the first time, darling.' I've seen these people at work. They came down to Deal one summer to film scenes from the life of Simon Raven. I was not impressed. I tell you, if I conducted my business that way, I'd have been on the parish years ago. For instance, they'll spend all morning filming some chap walking out through the French windows, pausing, and saying 'I've given Miranda a glass of warm milk. I think she'll sleep now', before exiting to the rose garden. All morning! And the chances are when you go to see the film that particular gem won't even be in it.

Well, if they want to waste their own time and money, that's their business; but I hate to see them fouling up the lives of ordinary, decent people.

'Have nothing to do with it,' I said. 'They'll set up their camera on the pitch, probably right on a length, while their underlings are doing unspeakable things in the hedges.'

'But, Gussy,' said Hewitson, 'I thought it would be rather fun.'

Fun! I was wasting my time. Obviously Hewitson was determined to allow the heathen hordes on to the sacred turf no matter what anyone said. He was deaf to reason. I made up my mind then and there to keep as far away as possible from the whole disagreeable business – unless, of course, there was anything I could do to help.

Hewitson very pointedly didn't ask me to go up for the filming. This may have been out of consideration for my feelings, but I doubt it. I believe he saw himself on the television screen, leading out the home side, cracking jokes with the stars, all that nonsense. He simply didn't want to share any of the glamour with an old friend. That's what I thought.

Shortly after this it occurred to me that I hadn't seen my Aunt Goronwy for about eleven years. She's not really my aunt, and we've never got on, but one does have responsibilities. At that time she lived at Cleethorpes and it struck me that in order to reach her I would have to travel within a few miles of Hilton Cupid. I had quite forgotten my conversation with Dudley Hewitson, so you may imagine my astonishment when, driving into the sleepy little village, I found it littered with large vans bearing the name of Viking Television. Could it be, I wondered, that this was the day when the filming was to take place? Hewitson had mentioned some date around this time, but I don't keep a note of other people's business.

I drove up to Trodds and found the place seething with young men in T-shirts. These were wandering about aimlessly with pieces of wire, sandwiches, clipboards, trousers, tape measures and beverages in paper cups. I realized almost at once that some of them were young women.

Hewitson was in the garden. He was surprised to see me. Perhaps surprised is the wrong word. At the sound of my voice he spun round like a man caught trying on another man's batting gloves. His expression darkened instantly and I was forced to the opinion that he thought my appearance in Hilton Cupid that day was the result of a calculated plot. Even when I pointed out that my arrival was total coincidence he still seemed to crackle with anger. I attempted to soothe him by drawing his attention to the fact that I know a thing or two about the film racket. I said I might actually be of help.

His reaction surprised me.

'You're not staying?'

'Of course,' I reassured him. 'I wouldn't leave an old friend in the lurch, I'm not like that. This is going to be a difficult day for everybody. I want to shoulder some of the burden. While you're getting the pitch marked I'll go and find the chap in charge.'

'But, Gussy . . .'

'I understand these people,' I said. 'I speak their language.'

The director was called Logan Hodge and I found him in the saloon bar of the Owl and Trumpet. He was a tall man with crinkly hair whitening at the edges. He put me in mind not so much of de Mille as of our old woodwork teacher. My spirits sank. With him was a smallish person muffled in cardigans, which struck me as odd on such a beautiful day.

'I'm Withers,' I said. 'I'm the liaison supremo.'

'I thought we'd got one of those already,' said Hodge.

'You mean Hewitson. Well, I've just left him. Don't think he's going to be a lot of help. On the verge of a nervous breakdown if you ask me. No, it'll be best if you channel everything through me.'

The man in the cardigans sneezed.

'Roger's got a cold,' said Hodge.

'Why isn't he in bed?' I asked.

'In bed? He's the leading man. He's in all the scenes we've come here to shoot. Roger Buckmaster is the star of the show.'

I promise you, I've never seen anyone who looked less like a cricketer than Roger Buckmaster. Under the woollies lurked your typical 'Play for Today' cuckolded husband or cowardly infantry officer. His large dark eyes were filled with fear and fluid. Frankly I could not see this pathetic creature stepping into line and driving the fast medium pacers through the covers. As for hooking the short ball

. . . well, the idea was laughable.

I drew the director to one side and lowered my voice.

'Couldn't you get someone else?' I suggested. 'I mean, the wretched chap's probably running a temperature . . .'

Hodge's pale blue eyes seemed to spring out at me.

'Someone else! Roger Buckmaster's the biggest switch-on in British television. To say nothing of the fact that we've already recorded nine-tenths of the programme. You don't seem to know the first thing about this business.'

I was about to point out that I was at school with a close personal friend of Ivor Langmuir's stand-in during the making of *The Smugglers of Madman's Cove*, when the orphan in the cocoon burst into a fit of coughing and had to be comforted with ginger wine. I turned away sadly. If this day's work ever got out, ever came to be seen in Australia for instance, the good name of English cricket would be damned. I nearly decided to wash my hands of the whole thing, but Hewitson and the others were depending on me. I had to stick it out.

I thought it would be wise to make friends with the unit overseer or whatever grandiose title they gave to the unhappy man who kept on shouting 'Quiet, please!' His name was Curly Griggs and he seemed totally ignorant on the subject of (a) the game of cricket, (b) the art of film making, and (c) the strength of the local beer. Clearly we couldn't count on much help from that quarter. The cameraman was a very different basket of vipers. I suspected he wasn't English, at least not completely, despite being called Lawrence Longman-Rivers. He had the cool, superior manner one associates with people whose parents have spent a long time abroad. Not that I wish to criticize such people, nor indeed their parents. But he had an abruptness that reminded me of Hassan Penfold, the old Devonshire leg-spinner. For instance, in the middle of my explanation of the difference between mid-wicket and wide mid-on he broke in with some irrelevant anecdote recalled from the days when he played for the Wiltshire Seconds. There was no need for that. All he had to do was mention that he had once played cricket and knew roughly what the fieldsmen were called. After all, the Wiltshire Seconds aren't what you'd call the cream. And he wasn't able to produce a signed scorecard or anything of that sort to back up this rather wild claim. Personally I don't remember a Longman-Rivers playing for Wiltshire, Firsts or Seconds.

The landlord of the Owl and Trumpet, a local man, was having a hard day. His beautiful public house was filled with braying Londoners ordering Campari Sodas and Vodka Tokays, drinks he couldn't even spell let alone serve. I grabbed a ham sandwich and a glass of Old Rookery ale and went outside into the sunshine. Here I met Hugo Nordquist, the young actor playing the part of Hilary Peacock's brother. I won't bore you with a synopsis of the story – its improbability is only exceeded by its tedium – but it might help if I mention that Nigel (Roger Buckmaster) is in pursuit of Annabel (Hilary Peacock) who believes she is the reincarnation of Hiffi, a Saxon princess. What any of this has to do with cricket I'm quite unable to tell you. Enquiries should be addressed to Eric Plank, the brilliant young author who dreamed up the whole thing, no doubt while under the influence.

Nordquist and I finished our drinks and strolled over to the pitch. During our chat about lift and spin he mentioned that Buckmaster had recently uncoupled himself from his wife and was now committed to a lady who trained wild animals. Also, that Miss Peacock had just rediscovered the Great Umpire – whose Word is final – and was eager to pass on her news to all and sundry. Nordquist himself claimed to be a Hindu but I think he was pulling my leg.

I ran Hewitson down in the garden. He had changed into his whites but was looking edgy. He turned on me angrily.

'Gussy,' he said, 'please don't go around upsetting the artists. They're under a great deal of pressure.'

Artists! Was he referring to the wife-beating, animal-trainer-loving little squirt who was about to bring the whole game of cricket into disrepute?

'I expressed concern for the man's health,' I said, 'though why I bothered I don't know. But have you actually seen him lift a bat? Personally I doubt if he could.'

'That's entirely beside the point,' snapped Hewitson. 'He's here to act, not to play. The most important scene takes place behind the pavilion between him and some woman.'

'She's a religious maniac.'

'It doesn't matter, Gussy. It's their business, not ours. And it's certainly not yours. I honestly can't think what you're doing here at all!'

Flecks of foam began to appear on his lips so I left him. In the drive I stopped a young hermaphrodite and asked it where everybody was.

'Lunch,' said the creature, and pointed to a ramshackle vehicle from whose gaping side other hermaphrodites were extracting plates of food.

'And when does the work start?' I enquired.

It looked at me as if I'd uttered an obscenity and hurried off.

Curly Griggs was standing by the wicket. He was drunk, there was no doubt about that. He couldn't even remember my name. We were joined by Longman-Rivers carrying round his neck what I took to be a mouth organ on a piece of string.

'Roger will have to bat at this end,' he said, pointing to the nearest stumps.

'What, all the time?' I asked.

'Yes,' he said.

'Suppose the other chap runs one off the first ball?'

'I don't know what you're talking about,' said the cameraman.

'I'm talking about cricket, that game which you claim to have played some years ago.'

I'd touched a nerve, I knew that. The corners of his mouth sank into his face. I realized I'd made an enemy, but I'm one of those people who simply has to speak his mind. It's the way I'm made. Longman-Rivers pretended not to hear. He walked to the stumps and held his mouth organ in the air. He then looked very hard at the mouth organ, took a step back and gazed around the field. It was at this moment I realized it wasn't a mouth organ at all. He'd obviously been watching the Test umpires and had come armed with a light meter. I do know that photographical people sometimes use these mechanical aids, but surely not when the sun is blazing down from a clear sky? I mean, if you can't see the ball under those conditions then you're never going to.

People were now assembling around the pavilion. Most of them were of the technical variety, but some were obviously members of the village team; cricketers, decent people. They kept themselves to themselves as one would expect of men properly brought up. While all around was confusion and argument the men in white quietly spat on their hands and waited.

The arrival of the director was the cue for everyone to break for tea. Buckmaster emerged shakily from the pavilion. He wore a large overcoat, several scarves and a fur hat of the type favoured by members of the Politburo. Somehow it didn't look right for cricket. He and Hodge, now joined by Griggs and Longman-Rivers, walked slowly out to the middle. What on earth they had to say to each other I can't imagine. Not one of them was competent to give an opinion about what the ball might do, and what else does one discuss when staring at the wicket?

As chance would have it, I'd packed my whites before setting off that morning. I don't know why; it's just one of those things one does between May and the first week in September. Emergencies do arise, like the one that now faced me. I changed in the gentleman's lavatory at the Owl and Trumpet then made my way back to the pitch, where I was able to mingle with the other players. The Cupidians thought I was a film-maker, and the film-makers thought I was a cricketer. I got one or two odd looks but I've come to expect that over the years.

Hewitson now arrived. He found a suitable spot in front of the pavilion, halted, peered around like a pheasant looking for its mate, and clapped his hands.

'All my people here, please,' he called briskly. 'Nice and smartly, if you wouldn't mind. There's a lot to do.'

I lurked on the edge of the village group, intrigued to know how Hewitson intended deceiving his players into wasting their time.

'We're here today,' he began, 'to help our friends from Viking Television in what I think is a terribly exciting project. We've all seen Roger Buckmaster and Hilary Peacock on the box. Today they've come amongst us to shoot scenes for the forthcoming production of *The Passions of Annabel*. I think that's rather thrilling, don't you?'

He paused to observe the excitement taking his men in its grip. They for their part did a terrific job in controlling themselves. There was no reaction at all. If any of them had ever come across the names Buckmaster or Peacock they hid it magnificently. Hewitson hurried on.

'There won't be much actual cricket played. Quite a bit of standing about, so I'm told. Filming's like that; rather technical. But I know you'll give the Viking people every assistance, and I've been authorized to reveal that afterwards Mr Hodge will be on duty in the public bar of the Owl, ready to . . . ha-ha . . . take orders!'

I almost felt embarrassed for the man. One measly glass of Old Rookery in return for a whole summer's day cast upon the water! As I turned away in shame a great voice smote us.

'Everybody in the middle of the field, please.'

It was Curly Griggs using one of those infernal amplified trumpet things.

'*Could* we buck up please? We're wasting time. Cricketing gentleman, *please*!'

Post-alcoholic irritation was clearly detectable in Griggs' voice, plus a nasty note of scorn. Obviously the locals were already cast as the nitwits and time wasters. From this moment on every artistic and technical act of incompetence would bring down abuse on the heads of the local stalwarts. I'd seen it all before.

The first shot required by Hodge was of Buckmaster walking down the pavilion steps. Not a great problem, one would have thought. Cricketers do it all their lives without thinking, even quite young cricketers, but for Hodge, Buckmaster and Longman-Rivers it threw up difficulties of incredible proportions.

'We shall need more light,' said the cameraman. 'The front of the pavilion's in shadow.'

One of the cricketers began to explain that it was built this way on purpose, and was immediately exiled to the boundary.

'Should I carry the bat in the left hand or the right?' enquired the David Garrick of the greensward.

'Curly, can we clear that mob away from the front of the pavilion?' demanded Hodge, ignoring the star of the show.

'Roger's got gloves of different colours. Does that matter?' asked Griggs.

'Is it possible to *move* the pavilion?' enquired the cameraman.

'Left hand or right hand?' repeated Buckmaster.

'Why isn't Hilary here?' Hodge wished to know, as if her presence would solve the problems of light, gloves, mob, etc. 'Can someone fetch her, now, please?'

'The pavilion's concreted into the ground,' came the pathetic voice of Hewitson. 'And there are pipes and things . . .'

'Look, let's try one,' suggested Hodge in desperation.

'We're going to try one,' bellowed Griggs. His tone intimated that this was a really novel idea, never before encountered by film-makers.

'We do need more light,' insisted Longman-Rivers.

'It might be fun seeing Roger emerging from the gloom,' said Hodge, clutching at straws.

'Bloody side-splitting,' muttered a quiet Lincolnshire voice, which was the cue for all the other cricketers to be exiled to the boundary.

'We're going to go for one,' continued Hodge. 'Curly, we've still got that rabble in front of the pavilion.'

'Look, I've asked you once,' came Curly's amplified voice. 'Please move. We're wasting time.'

Then Buckmaster, 'Logan, did you say left hand?'

'The light's diabolical.'

'Has anyone actually *seen* Hilary today?'

'Everybody's got to move, madam. Everybody!'

It took ten minutes to move the local peasantry from the place they always occupied on match days. They were not pleased. Suddenly there was nowhere to go, except home, so that's where they went. I knew that later they would be required, but would not be available.

During the displacement of the multitude large electricians had been erecting powerful lights to shine on to the front of the pavilion. Hodge suddenly saw them.

'I said I *didn't* want lights!' he screamed.

'You'll never see Roger without lights,' explained the cameraman.

'I don't *want* to see him!'

'You don't want what?' asked Buckmaster, who had only caught a part of the dialogue.

'Anyone not involved in this scene please keep very quiet,' bellowed Curly.

'When we've killed those lights we'll go for a take,' said Hodge firmly.

'This is impossible!' snapped Longman-Rivers, stamping his foot.

He and Hodge now had a blistering row somewhere in the region of long-off. It lasted about seven minutes. Blows were not exchanged, but it was a close thing.

'No lights,' muttered the cameraman furiously as he rejoined his minions, and I guessed that his displeasure would reverberate for many months in the marble halls of Viking Television. Careers would be put in jeopardy, and the film itself would be a disaster. But I had known that from the beginning.

'We'll go for a take,' said Hodge smugly.

A moody silence fell across the field. The camera purred. Buckmaster emerged from the pavilion.

'Cut!' called Hodge. 'That was lovely. Perfect. All right for you, Lawrence?'

'Perfect,' said the cameraman. 'Couldn't see a thing. Beautiful.'

'Couldn't see what?' enquired Buckmaster.

'You looked like Everton Weekes coming in to bat at three in the morning. Smashing.'

Again cameraman and director withdrew to long-off. The exchange of views was briefer than before, and I suspect that Longman-Rivers was pointing out some of the cruder Laws of Nature; for instance, 'If I can't see the actors you haven't got a film. If you haven't got a film, you may find you haven't got a job.' As they wandered back Longman-Rivers called out,

'We'll have all the lights back, Jacko.'

This exercise took about a quarter of an hour. I've no doubt the whole thing could have been done in three and a half minutes if there'd been a suitable reward for doing so. But there wasn't, so it didn't.

Hodge did three more takes of Buckmaster descending the pavilion steps. They all looked very boring to me, but apparently one of them had more feeling than the others. Perhaps I should have pointed out to Hodge that Buckmaster was wearing two left pads, but I didn't want to hold up the shooting.

Next we had a shot of Buckmaster arriving at the wicket. For this we needed the local players who were to be grouped picturesquely in a phalanx behind the wicket.

'Can we have all the cricketing gentlemen on the field, please?' bawled Curly Griggs through his machine. 'As quickly as possible. We're running a little behind.'

Several of the Cupidians were sound asleep in the long grass and had to be shaken. One or two had vanished, never to be seen again. To cover their absence I attached myself to the group. Hodge approached us warily, rather like a man meeting his first tribe of cannibals.

'That,' he said, pointing, 'is the camera. Mr Buckmaster will enter the shot *here*. When I call "action" you all begin to act. That is to say, don't act, behave normally, but don't just stare.'

Curly had the job of placing the field.

'Can we have two of you here, three there, three behind, and two just to the left?'

I really couldn't let this pass.

'If you have ten players in a segment between the wicket-keeper and backward square leg you commit two blunders,' I said. 'In the first place, it's not allowed. Secondly you will create the impression that we have thirty or forty fielders operating at the same time, which is also against the rules.'

The look of blank anger on Griggs' face told me that *The Laws of Cricket* was not his constant pillow book.

'Thank you, Mr Withers,' he said icily. 'I shall make a note of that at the first opportunity. Meanwhile would you like to go where you're bloody told, and shut up!'

I was obviously dealing with a retardee. I didn't hold it against him. In fact I had to admit that he'd done jolly well to get any sort of work at all, not that being chief shouter to an idiot like Hodge was exactly the dizzy heights. I took up my position at fifth backward short leg and waited.

Hodge was staring at us miserably.

'Don't all bunch together,' he called.

We, the cricketers, exchanged uneasy glances.

Griggs said, 'Spread out a bit.'

We spread out a bit.

Hodge said, 'Not that far. We'll never see you if you wander all over the field.'

'Close in a bit,' said Griggs.

We closed in a bit.

'Now you're bunching again!' shouted Hodge. 'Look, can we have a bit of co-operation, for Pete's sake?'

The men of Hilton Cupid glanced in my direction. I took this to mean that they had appointed me their spokesman. I could understand why.

'Sir,' I began, in the belief that courtesy always pays even when addressed to barbarians, 'either you allow us to field where God intended, or you hammer little yellow pegs into the ground to indicate exactly where you want us. We don't mind which. We're here to help.'

Longman-Rivers, who must have been otherwise occupied during this, now looked in our direction.

'They're too bunched up,' he said.

'I *know* they're too bunched up!' snapped Hodge.

'And there are too many of them.'

'I'm perfectly well aware of that, thank you very much! Curly, let's lose most of them.'

At last, something that Curly was good at!

'You, you and you,' he barked, but already most of the real players had drifted back to the long grass and dreams of cricket. I and two others remained, the wicketkeeper and an elderly gentleman who, I learnt afterwards, had once performed opposite Lillian Williams in a production of *Knight of the Burning Pestle*.

Longman-Rivers was peering at us through his Brownie.

'I can't see them,' he said.

'You'll have to come much closer,' bawled Hodge. 'We can't see you if you stand miles away.'

'I still can't see them,' said the cameraman.

Hodge, desperate now, charged towards us.

'Look, can we all try and work together, for God's sake? When I say closer, I don't mean three inches closer. I mean *here*!'

He manhandled me into a position where my left toe was actually touching the popping crease. I protested.

'Quite apart from matters of legality, which obviously don't bother you in the least, I stand a very good chance of being injured by that bat.'

'He's not going to play a shot,' hissed Hodge.

'How do you know?'

'Because it says so in the script, Mr Withers!'

'Does the audience know that?' I asked. 'If not, they'll think I'm an absolute fool standing as close as this.'

'Can you think of any way in which we can prevent that happening?' screamed Hodge, his face now very red and his hair slightly more silvery. 'Right,' he continued, 'if nobody objects we shall go for a little take!'

This turned out to be eleven little takes. We had Buckmaster sneezing at the crucial moment, then a hair in the gate (which, as I'm sure you know, means that the contents of an old sofa has somehow got between the lens and the film.) This was followed by a fit of coughing and more hairs in the gate. Next, I really did have to point out that Buckmaster was wearing two left pads. Also, that he had been given a Harrow cap to wear which, bearing in mind the criminal nature of the character he was playing, might have resulted in litigation.

At last, having got this scene in the can (and the best place for it) we moved on to the shot of Nordquist running up and bowling. Surely no problem here? He was a fit young man and looked splendid in his spotless whites. The one snag was that Nordquist had no idea how to bowl. He said he'd seen it done and was prepared to have a go, but he'd never actually done it. Hodge, showing great control, suggested he tried one.

Nordquist's approach to the wicket would have earned him high marks in any tango dancing contest. On arriving at the stumps he stopped dead, paused, raised his hand above his head as if reaching for a strap in a Tube, then flung the ball very hard. I said he was fit. The ball cleared the batsman's stumps by about thirty feet, still rising, and finally disappeared into the orchard adjoining the cricket pitch.

A cathedral silence fell across our activities. The expression on Hodge's face suggested a Russian landowner who has just been told about the Revolution. There was stoicism there, even courage, but tragedy dominated. Nordquist, like Buckmaster, was already immortalized in many hours of expensively recorded programme. He could not be replaced. Neither could he bowl, a function crucial to the plot.

I realized at once that this was not the moment to take refuge in anonymity. The boat was speeding towards the rocks. Someone had to seize the tiller.

'Give me ten minutes with him in the nets,' I said. 'I don't guarantee he'll finish up opening for England, but perhaps we can sort something out.'

'Take ten,' said Hodge hoarsely.

'We're taking ten,' bellowed Griggs, obviously cross that the hour had produced the man, and that the man was me.

Forty-five minutes later I'd managed to get Nordquist to run more or less in the way agreed by the rest of humanity – that is, forward, one foot after the other. But I had not managed to get him to run on past the stumps, or to swing his arm over, or to release the ball in approximately the right direction. We both worked very hard. The will was there but in the end I had to confess that the task was a trifle more difficult than teaching a horse to knit.

I discovered Hodge in the showers, sitting on the floor. He looked older. I lowered my voice.

'Suppose we get a stand-in, and shoot the rest of the scene from the top of the church tower?'

I don't know if he heard me. He was muttering to himself all the while, something about suspending Nordquist's agent by the fly buttons over a vat of boiling curry. I tip-toed away.

Longman-Rivers and Griggs were lying in the grass discussing the pitfalls inherent in the Two No-Trumps opening bid. I was sickened. It was the nearest thing I'd ever seen to the Children of Israel dancing round the Golden Calf. No wonder Moses had lost his temper! I looked them straight in the eye.

'I have just left Mr Hodge,' I said. 'He is not a well man. However, he was just about to tell me that he thought we should shoot the scene with stand-ins. So, if you would be good enough to transport your camera to the top of the church tower I will arrange things on the pitch.'

They didn't believe me, that was clear. If they'd had an inch of gut between them, they'd have laughed in my face. But of course they didn't. Perhaps the chance of removing themselves a long way from the cricket pitch was too tempting to resist.

'Good idea,' drawled Longman-Rivers. 'Better get cracking before the light goes.'

Having taken charge, I was in no mood to pussyfoot with the minor characters. I'd lost most of my real cricketers so was forced to recruit hangers-on, clipboard-huggers, etc. I ordered seven of them into whites. On Hewitson I conferred the honour of bowling. He's no good at it, but at least he can go through the motions. When it came to batting we were desperately short, so I assumed that responsibility myself. I sent Buckmaster to the non-striker's end, placed the field, then waved my handkerchief at the distant figures on top of the church tower. On receiving the agreed response, the waving of a different-coloured handkerchief, I called 'play' and Hewitson began his run.

The Passions of Annabel reached our screens in the middle of January. At this time of the year I'm normally hard at work polishing my leg-glide and off-cutter at the Indira Gandhi Indoor Cricket School. But curiosity overcame duty, and I set aside one hour each Friday evening to see what all the fuss had been about. Episodes One to Six were a total waste of time. People stared into one another's eyes, lost their tempers, burst into tears, and generally behaved badly. I awarded Roger Buckmaster 1½ out of 10 for acting, which is higher than I'd mark him for cricket. Hilary Peacock turned out to have a face like Sir Edward Elgar and the sort of voice that sends dogs running under tables. Hugo Nordquist was good. In one scene he blacked Buckmaster's eye, and in another fell off a horse with complete conviction. I had the same sensation watching him sprawling in the mud that one has watching a youngster cracking the short ball away to the boundary. One to watch for the future.

In Episode Seven there was talk of a cricket match. In Episode Eight even more talk and a quick glimpse of a pair of cricket boots. The series was improving. Episode Nine took us to the broad acres of Lord Something-or-other. A cricket match had been arranged. After a lot of nonsense in somebody's bedroom we had a shot – Scene 1, Take 4 as I remember – showing Roger Buckmaster descending the pavilion steps. Then, before I could reach for my box of after-dinner mints, we were back in London again. That was it. Scene 1, Take 4. Six and a half seconds of an unrecognizable Roger Buckmaster walking down three wooden steps. Where was Scene 2? And, far more to the point, where was Scene 3? Where was the hauntingly lovely panorama encapsulating the heartbreaking beauty of an English summer day, with me batting? Where?

I telephoned Hewitson the next morning. He was cool, and I got the impression he somehow held me responsible for the non-appearance of himself and his chums on television. Me, the one person who had held the whole shoddy thing together! I was speechless, which allowed Hewitson to make a telling remark.

'One thing's certain, Gussy,' he said. 'I'll never do it again. I'll never allow a film unit within a hundred miles of the place in future. If only I'd known what it was going to be like, if only someone had said . . . Oh! Sorry, must dash.'

I'm glad he rang off at that moment. I was on the verge of breaking the principle of a lifetime (people get so unreasonable when you say 'I told you so!') and I didn't want to get into a row with Dudley Hewitson. After all, he *is* one of my best friends.

8

The People's Choice

Professional sportsmen, like jugglers, fire-eaters and other entertainers, should be wary about expressing their political opinions. For instance, if you, a cricket lover, happen also to be a raving fascist you're unlikely to thrash your hands to pieces in appreciation of a cover drive executed by a confessed Marxist. The political devil inside you will whisper that the stroke was not as good as many you've seen, that the delivery was the kindest of half-volleys, and that anyhow one goodish shot doesn't make up for all the indifferent ones that preceded it. A cricketer of the wrong hue has to perform better than Dr Grace, Bradman, Hobbs and Hutton combined if he wishes to be appreciated by spectators of the right hue. However, if the aforesaid stroke had been struck by someone sharing your own narrow prejudices, you would have been dancing in your seat and throwing money. Of such stuff are we made.

Happily, this frightful intolerance does not work the other way round. Cricketers don't mind who watches. They don't even mind who plays with them, which is tolerance taken to the point of saintliness. I once played in a match where first slip happened to be an anarchist. He had a superb pair of hands and it was a privilege to appear on the greensward with him, though I must say the conversation in the shower afterwards left a lot to be desired. I was accused of 'social breaking and entering' simply because I owned the boots I'd been wearing. His boots, he said, belonged to the world. Anyone who cared to could wear them – which, considering their size, shape and condition, I thought was a fairly empty gesture. When I mentioned his three remarkable catches – one an absolute fizzer – he said congratulations were not in order. He'd done it for the people, he said. What about the three batsmen concerned? I said. Yes, them too, he said. This answer confused me, so I left the shower even though I hadn't quite finished.

However, I stick to my first point. Politics and cricket are best pursued in different arenas, representing as they do two quite unrelated philosophies. Cricket is about the individual doing his best for others. Politics is about hitting impertinent journalists for six and stumping the chaps on the opposite front bench. For example, take Andrew Larrimore, the Member for the area around Pottingly. If I told you he was a Conservative, you wouldn't be in the least surprised. Pottingly is a charming little rural spot, tucked away among the greenery like a robin's egg. But if I went on to tell you that Mr Larrimore's majority was wafer-thin, you might raise an eyebrow. It was all to do with the change of boundaries – constituency boundaries, that is. In the great shake-up Larrimore had lost forty square miles of ancient pastures and retired colonels, and gained row upon row of boot and shoe operatives, thus turning what had been a safe billet into a bed of nails.

Andrew Larrimore was a jolly nice chap. He had played stool ball for the Twelfth Hussars, and now sat on the board of Messrs Hirst and Larrimore, the Stripford brewers. 'Murder your Thirst with a Hirst' is as familiar a saying in those parts as *Ich Dien* is in Wimbledon. He had a lovely wife and four lovely children and a quite adorable bank manager. The only blot on the page was that wretched three-figure majority that threatened his membership of the Parliamentary Stool Ball Club.

People with Mr Larrimore's predicament have only one course to follow. They must get out, get seen, and, if possible, get loved. Open every fête in sight; take part in every sponsored run, hop, skip, jump, etc; shake hands with everything that moves, and get their picture in the local paper every week without fail. If strictly followed this treatment will ensure that, come election time, at least eight more people will vote for you than would otherwise have been the case. It's hard work, it's boring, and it's vaguely humiliating, but if politics is your game then that's what you have to do.

Also, if you're lucky, your friends will give you a hand. Andrew Larrimore had a friend. His name was Julian Yewsley and he lived in a large house on the edge of Pottingly village. He was also captain of the cricket team. His contribution was to suggest that the Member took part in the annual Pottingly *v.* Uxcombe cricket match. Bags of useful exposure there, said Yewsley. When Larrimore pointed out that he knew as little about cricket as he did about funding the National Debt, Yewsley didn't turn a hair. He'd give him a few tips, he said. Anyhow, he wouldn't be asked to bowl, or field near the wicket, or bat higher than last. In fact, he probably wouldn't have to bat at all, and if the worst came to the worst he could always rush from the field in response to some fictitious summons from the Mother of Parliaments.

Before hurtling on, a few words about the Pottingly *v.* Uxcombe fixture might be helpful. The boundaries of the two villages adjoined but, like many neighbouring communities, they didn't get on. Uxcombe church was larger and older than Pottingly's, but Pottingly Manor was considerably grander than Uxcombe House, and so on. Pottingly was smaller, wealthier, snobbier. Uxcombe had a history of belligerence. In the eighteenth century, while the peasants of Pottingly were plagued with frontal baldness from continually tugging their forelocks, the labourers of Uxcombe were being shipped in crates to Australia for dumb insolence. Time had mellowed the relationship a little, and there were even cases of intermarriage between the two tribes, but it didn't take much – an imagined insult, a tactless display of riches – to stir up old feelings.

Of course, the one event guaranteed to keep the wound green was the annual match, and had Mr Larrimore been better informed he might have declined the invitation to involve himself in this Stone Age argument. Had he been shrewder he might have realized that Yewsley, friend though he claimed to be, was employing him for the purpose of getting one up on the old enemy. The deviousness of the tactic was not lost on the Uxcombe committee. As soon as word reached them that Pottingly had stooped to including a politician in their team, they immediately set to work to find a better, that is to say a more alarming, politician of their own.

This wasn't easy. Politicians either come large and famous, in which case they treat one's invitations with contempt, or else they come small and undistinguished and one can do without them. But Hubert Lockhart, the Uxcombe skipper, had a brainwave. In the back streets of Stripford there lived a man who not only played a bit of cricket but also had a sinister reputation in the area of politics. His name was Desmond Claud Carew and he had several times stood as the Marxist Fishermen's candidate in Eastbourne. He had also once scored 112 for the Huntingdonshire Schoolboys. Carew was no longer young, and his lean body was wracked from years of speech-making outside the Cavendish Hotel, but Lockhart suspected that the sight of a paid-up Conservative fielding at extra cover would cause the blood to surge and the muscles to flex as of old.

As the day of the match approached, Andrew Larrimore began to regret his quixotic gesture. Not only was he a duffer at the game itself, he was also worried about his appearance. Some men seem made for whites; others turn out looking like Morris dancers or hospital porters. Larrimore was in the second category. Also, rumours were getting back to him concerning the true nature of the match. Not only was he going to have to cope with a hard ball and jester's motley, he was also getting caught up in an inter-village feud which would win him few political medals. He would have phoned Yewsley and pleaded illness, but already a poster had been drawing-pinned to the old ash outside the church announcing his participation in the grisly business. To chicken out now would be to lose a whole basketful of votes.

The Friday before the game was warm and dry with a good forecast for the weekend. Larrimore was livid, but Saturday began more promisingly. The skies were grey and a light shower fell like the quality of mercy on Larrimore beneath. He arrived at the Yewsley residence for lunch exuding a bogus keenness. 'Just a light sprinkling,' he declared, loud enough for any passing voter to hear. 'Won't last.' Much to his alarm, it didn't. The rain stopped at one, and by a quarter to two an impish sun was grinning down on Pottingly as if it had never had an evil thought in its head.

Yewsley then said that it might be a good idea if Larrimore popped into the Crooked Billet before the match and bought a drink for one or two of the opposition. Secretly he hoped that the sight of a real, live Member of Parliament would alarm them. It was a long shot but Yewsley was prepared to try anything. Out loud he said that a discreet show of generosity was worth a hundred and fifty votes in that part of the world. Larrimore wasn't enthusiastic. He saw himself being taken gross advantage of by louts who, at election time, would gleefully tear his posters from the hedges. But how could he refuse?

Larrimore managed to delay the departure to the pub by spending twenty minutes in the bathroom, and by the time he and Yewsley arrived the place was almost empty. The landlord was drinking a cup of tea – never a boisterous sight – and in a distant corner a pair of lovers were gazing into each other's eyes as if the secret of life was written there in tiny print. There was only one person at the bar itself, a lean, brown-faced man in his fifties. He wore a threadbare tweed jacket and a scruffy pair of off-white flannel trousers. A cricketer? It seemed possible. Larrimore and Yewsley approached the bar.

'Good afternoon, landlord,' beamed Larrimore. 'Two pints of your excellent bitter, please, and . . .', half turning to the possible cricketer, '. . . whatever our friend is drinking.'

'Our friend' was nursing a large gin and tonic. He drained the glass and pushed it across the bar.

'Mr Andrew Larrimore?' enquired D. C. Carew in a voice every bit as cultivated as Larrimore's.

'Er, yes. I'm afraid I . . .'

'Thought you'd be turning up here sooner or later. That's why I hung on.'

'You're Mr . . . er . . .?'

'Will you be bowling this afternoon?'

'I very much doubt it,' smiled Larrimore.

'Pity. I was looking forward to that. Still, you'll be batting.'

'Pretty low down, probably,' said Larrimore.

D. C. Carew reached for his refilled glass.

'But you *will* be fielding?'

'Yes, of course. Not too near the action, but fielding, certainly.'

'In that case I shall find you, never fear. Thank you for the refreshment.'

He drank up quickly and left. Larrimore looked puzzled.

'Who the devil was that?'

'No idea,' said Yewsley. 'Mind you, they're all a bit peculiar over in Uxcombe.'

'What did he mean by "find me"?'

'God knows. I wouldn't give it another thought. They're a rum crowd over there.'

The match started on the dot, and from the first ball was conducted in a spirit that would have been wholly appropriate to a fixture between the Montagues and the Capulets. Every mean underhand trick was resorted to, every device that fell just short of breaking the Laws, plus one or two that didn't. The slips jingled coins as the ball left the bowler's hand, and the batsmen continually called for the sight screens to be moved, one foot to the right, three inches to the left.

Uxcombe batted first and, considering everything, did rather well. At 52 for 2 they seemed set for a useful total. Then came a collapse. Lockhart, the Uxcombe skipper, attributed this to the ball being changed following the loss, or alleged loss, of the original one. At 71 for 6 things looked bleak for the visitors, but the scales of fortune were about to tilt once more. To the wicket now came the lean, brown-faced D. C. Carew. It was immediately obvious to the knowledgeable that this man had played before. He took possession of the crease like someone who had already scored fifty, had departed briefly to replace a broken boot-lace, and now intended to get the rest of his century. His glance around the field was cursory and dismissive, his stance unfussy. The first ball he played gently back to the bowler. The second he hit for four. The third, too. As the bowler raced in to deliver the next ball the fielder at close backward short leg sneezed violently. Carew took one pace to the off and cracked the ball hard at the sneezer. It struck the wretched man full on the shin and the match was held up for several minutes while cold compresses were applied.

One of those who hurried forward to give succour was the local Member. He knew next to nothing about the human body but people don't vote for chaps who hang about in the deep while other chaps lie bleeding. As the medical party returned to the pavilion and the fielders to their positions, D. C. Carew's hooded gaze followed the figure of the People's Choice to the deepest and finest of deep fine legs. So that's where they'd hidden him, mused the extreme left-winger. Excellent.

What followed can only be described as a cricketing equivalent of the Roman games. To begin with Carew was content to glance the ball finely to leg, wide enough to beat the keeper but straight enough to dismay the distinguished visitor on the boundary. Yewsley changed the bowling but Carew was equal to it. Whether at fine leg, or flexible third man, or nearly invisible deep mid-off, Carew unerringly fired the ball straight at Larrimore.

When the performance started everyone was rather amused, even the Pottingly players. The sight of our superiors making fools of themselves is always worth the price of admission. But as the torment went on and the score mounted, the smiles began to fade. A joke was a joke, but this was supposed to be cricket.

For Larrimore the basic trouble was the ball itself. It was so unnaturally hard, and it sped towards him so quickly it was often impossible to get out of the way. And when he did manage to step smartly to one side, in the fashion of a bullfighter avoiding the killing horns, he sensed his colleagues were not pleased. Well, too bad! If they thought he was going to risk a promising career that, in the fullness of time, might well see him surrounded by plain-clothes detectives, simply to put them one up in some futile village quarrel, they could think again.

He blamed Yewsley for the whole thing, Yewsley and the voters. Who the hell did they think he was? Some public entertainer, a sort of walking Aunt Sally who could be hired from the Palace of Westminster for the price of a lunch? Well, the inhabitants of Pottingly and Uxcombe, and Stripford itself, could think again. If they couldn't recognize a rising political star when they saw one, that was their bad luck. If necessary he would find himself a seat where the voters were a little more perceptive, and where cricket was regarded simply as a game, not as a ritual test of one's virility. If the local Association thought they could get a better man to fight this seat, then . . . Great God in Heaven!!

It almost hit him clean between the eyes. In his preoccupation he simply hadn't been looking – then suddenly, like some awful close-up in a film, there it was, inches from his face, round, red and detestable. With a gesture not uncontaminated by hints of terror, cowardice, surrender, etc., he flung up his hands. The ball thudded into the soft, fleshy palms . . . and stuck. He'd stopped the ball. But, no, not merely stopped it, he'd caught it. He, Andrew Larrimore, had caught the ball! He, A. P. W. Larrimore, M. P., had snatched the flying orb from the sky and dismissed a batsman. And not just *a* batsman – Desmond Claud Carew, Marxist of this parish and hitter extraordinary.

While the incredible beauty of the moment was wrapping itself round him like silk underwear the other fielders raced towards him, banged him on the back and declared it was the best catch they'd seen all season. In less time than it takes to say 'Made in India' the Member had become the most popular man in the constituency.

Several months later the Hon. Member for Stripford was called to speak during the debate that swirled and eddied around the Second Reading of the Garden Refuse (Mid-Wales) Bill. He had nothing to say about refuse or Mid-Wales, but he seized the attention of the House by his remarks on the subject of moral fibre. He said that what the country lacked was not garden incinerators but guts. If the youth of Britain, he said, would think less of themselves and more of the 'team' many of our problems would melt away. It was patience and dedication and, yes, old-fashioned courage that would put us back where we belonged – on top. Everybody in the House thought it was an excellent speech, though they weren't sure what it was about. Even in Pottingly they didn't know what it was about, but they thought it was a jolly good effort none the less, and timely.

9

Under the Flannel

I hate people who make fun of cricket. I detest those show-biz matches where crooners and banjo-pluckers presume to rub shoulders with real men, real players. In my opinion the only games that deserve attention are those where two teams are selected on merit. I don't wish to be entertained by a stream of questionable music-hall patter while trying to judge length and line. I like a joke, of course I do, but not out in the middle. Even the blackmail of a 'good cause' leaves me unmoved. There's a place for good causes, but it's certainly not on a cricket pitch.

Having said this, I have to confess I once allowed myself to be drawn into a disgraceful piece of nonsense. I was assured that the match would be played to a serious conclusion, and strictly by the Laws. Under these conditions I agreed to take part, but long before the sun sank that day I bitterly regretted my decision.

It was Horace Johnson's idea . . . something to do with raising money to mend the church tower. Johnson was skipper at Dingewall, a flat village on the Romney Marsh. The tower was notable because it acted as a beacon for travellers lost in that trackless waste. Neither lost travellers nor church towers mean much to me, but I owed Johnson a favour. Only the year before he'd very decently lent me a bootlace during one of the North Sea Gas qualifying matches – so, against every instinct, I said I'd play.

Having committed myself, I discovered we were all expected to wear silly clothes. The match was advertised as Good Chaps *v.* Bad Chaps and we all had to turn up appropriately dressed. Our team were the Bad Chaps.

Johnson, a bit of a fusser, asked us to let him know in good time which undesirable historical character we intended impersonating. I remembered I had Great Uncle Jack's swallow-tail coat in the attic, so plumped for Henri le Grillon, the distinguished French poisoner. But the next post brought new instructions. Apparently all the other players, Johnson included, had chosen to go as Kerry Packer – not so much a comment on the gentleman himself as a cheap way out of the costume problem. As a team of ten Kerry Packers and one French mass murderer would have caused confusion in the minds of the spectators, Johnson now enclosed a list of bad-hats from which we had to make our choice. All the usual people were there – Torquemada, Nero (how do you wear pads with a toga, over or under?), Genghis Khan; but no Lloyd George, interestingly, or King John.

I found it impossible to decide. Basically I'm a cricketer, pure and simple. The thought of trying to play the leg-glide festooned in scimitars and beads appalled me. The game's hard enough in ordinary flannels without dressing up. But Johnson's first letter was soon followed by a second. Again most of his players had gone for the easy option, in this case Dr Crippen. To resolve the matter Johnson had been forced to draw names out of a hat. He was pleased to inform me that I had drawn Ivan the Terrible.

For several days I was sick with dismay and pains in the feet. I really thought I'd have to cry off on doctor's orders, but the crisis passed. Fate, it seemed, had boxed my compass. There was nothing for it but to contact the Russian Cultural Attaché for advice on Ivan's manner of dress, length of beard etc. A few days later I was visited by two plain-clothes men, but they went away when I explained about Johnson and the church tower.

The game was arranged for the first Saturday in August. We had to report to Johnson's cottage before lunch and be ready to take the field, appropriately dressed, at two sharp. Several old friends were there. Baggy Baldwin, from school, slapped me on the back as I emerged from the green room declaring I didn't look in the least like J. Edgar Hoover. He, apparently, was Jack the Ripper, but to me he looked no different from normal. Billy Yardstone was there, from the Wanderers, dressed as Abdul the Mad, an unfortunate piece of casting. Yardstone worked for a building society and was shy to the point of invisibility. To see his small, haunted face peering out from under a jewelled turban brought a lump to my throat. Our best bat, Bully Huckstep, was well suited to the role of Genghis Khan, but I wondered how he would manage his flowing drives cluttered with cutlasses.

The biggest surprise of all was Johnson. I'd heard via the grapevine that he had been lucky enough to draw the name of Arthur Scargill, but the creature who called us all into the morning room for a pre-match briefing wore green tights, a yellow blouse and a red pointed hat with a bobble on it. If this was Johnson's idea of political satire, I said to myself, then I wanted no part of it. Surely they could mend their wretched tower without descending to lampoonery. But Johnson had a shock for us.

'I'm Rumpelstiltskin,' he said. 'We seemed to be short on evil gnomes so I stepped into the breach. From now until the end of the match we shall all address each other by our characters' names. Right. Batting order. Genghis Khan will open with Dr Goebbels, followed by myself, then Jack the Ripper, Frankenstein's monster, the Sheriff of Nottingham, Dr Crippen, Torquemada, Abdul the Mad, Nero and Ivan the Terrible.'

Typical! Dragged away from my normal Saturday routine; got up, at no little cost, like a raving lunatic; put in last! I've never claimed to be a great batsman but a casual glance through the records of several villages south of Tewkesbury will show that I'm not exactly a beginner. And don't be deceived by the occasional single-figure score. Those bland threes and fives often conceal a stubborn, match-turning fight. But those were real games; today's contest wasn't. Going in last was probably a blessing in disguise.

Luckily it was only a short walk to the Molecatcher's Arms, which overlooked the pitch. The landlord, an ex-blast-furnace-manager, flinched visibly as we entered the saloon bar. He had been put on his guard by Johnson, but the sight of Frankenstein's monster, bolt and all, ordering gins and dry sherries for the likes of Dr Crippen and Jack the Ripper must have made him wonder if perhaps he'd chosen the wrong profession. A television set gleamed greenly over the bar. It was England *v.* Australia, the last few overs before lunch. An ache seized me as I gazed at the clean young men in their spotless whites. I could have been there with my smoked salmon and a half-bottle of Moselle, applauding, gossiping with my neighbours, behaving in a civilized way. Instead, here I was with a beard down to my waist, wearing a stinking surplice that the man at the theatrical costumiers assured me was identical to the one worn by the unpopular boyar of the same name.

A few of the opposition began to arrive. I recognized Buddha, their skipper, and Henry V, but could not distinguish between St Francis of Assisi and the Venerable Bede. It occurred to me that the preponderance of churchmen on the other side – Bernard of Clairvaux had been pointed out to me, and St Augustine – might actually work in our favour. Batting and bowling in a habit was not going to be easy. This wouldn't affect J. S. Bach, but Richard the Lionheart's chainmail and St George's armour would be a definite hindrance, unless of course one of them was the wicketkeeper.

Rumpelstiltskin and Buddha went out and tossed. Buddha won and decided to bat. Our Dr Crippen was invited to open the attack from the pub end. Buddha himself went in first with J. S. Bach, a square-on insurance salesman from Hounslow. Crippen quickly found a length and managed to keep them fairly quiet, but they hammered Nero from the village end. Beneath the imperial sheets he was Grant Duxbury, a medium pacer who had once been knocking on the door of Cumbria Club and Ground. To see him struggling up to the wicket, blood-stained toga flying in all directions, was a tragic sight. He found it impossible to get a clean swing of the arm because of the cut of his chasuble. After three overs he flung down the ball and marched off angrily into the deep. He was replaced by Torquemada, leg-breaks and top-flippers.

Now, I don't claim to be an authority on the Spanish Inquisition, but I'll bet a fiver none of them wore Eldew's 'Grass-grabber' cricket boots. Torquemada, an estate agent, did. Also he lumbered Judge Jeffreys, the Bad Chap's umpire, with cloaks, knives, crucifixes, hats etc. Surely this was against the spirit of the match? I agree the game should never have been played in the first place but, having accepted the conditions, it was wrong to try to gain a mean advantage. Not surprisingly, he soon got Bach, J. S. (playing back to the fuller length ball) and had Buddha caught in the slips; 32 for 2. Henry V and Francis of Assisi didn't last long, but Bernard of Clairvaux, a retired member of the CID, and St George got their heads down and took no chances. At 57 for 4 Rumpelstiltskin was looking for the breakthrough that would tilt the match positively in our favour. Abdul the Mad was tried, but his curly shoes played havoc with his run-up. Frankenstein's monster kept hitting his bolt with his arm, and by now Crippen was puce with exhaustion.

So the ball was thrown to me.

My friends will tell you I have a fair variety of shots in my locker. The pitch was turning so I decided to let go with a little off-spin. The first two were sighters. The Sheriff of Nottingham, behind the stumps, made a ridiculous display of flinging himself full length to stop them – but Solomon, the umpire at my end, only just signalled them as wides. It was, however, my third delivery that caused all the trouble. I don't know how it happened – perhaps a trick of the wind or an errant nodule of gum arabic – but somehow the ball became attached to my beard and both were sent speeding down the wicket. Bernard of Clairvaux reared back as any man would confronted by a hearth rug travelling at over 30 mph. He lashed at it and, in the process, managed to touch the ball itself. This flew in a gentle arc and was caught by Jack the Ripper at square leg. We all appealed, casting our vestments into the air in enthusiasm. Solomon's finger was half-way up when Bernard counter-appealed on the grounds that the ball had been caught 'with the aid of the beard' (Law 44), which still clung to it. Solomon – something in groceries, I think – bit his lip and said 'Not out'.

We couldn't believe our ears. Rumpelstiltskin was livid, and I wasn't exactly enchanted. Agreed, the whiskers were marginally involved in the incident, but this was hardly a Test Match! We were all labouring under colossal difficulties and to invoke the small print of the Laws was indefensible. Particularly as Bernard of Clairvaux went on to make 112. They declared at tea, 281 for 6, and our lot were pretty tight-lipped, believe me.

Our innings began badly. Genghis Khan refused to leave his scimitar in the dressing-room and, stepping back to drive the ball through the covers, found two and a half feet of cold steel between his legs. He collapsed across his stumps and had to be treated for a cut toe. Rumpelstiltskin never got going and Jack the Ripper had a real brute that came back. Frankenstein's monster batted sensibly but, because of the size of his boots, failed to make a quick single and was run out. So, 42 for 4 and not much batting to come. The Sheriff of Nottingham was completely out of touch and Dr Crippen was given out, stumped. This was a highly dubious decision, handed down yet again by the weak as water Solomon under pressure from the wicketkeeper. Thus, 60 for 6!

Torquemada now joined Dr Goebbels, who had played an admirably straight bat from the beginning. In four overs they completely changed the complexion of the match.

The Inquisitor-General's first victim was the Venerable Bede, who up to then had taken 3 for 16. The scourge of heretics stepped fearlessly down the wicket and hit Bede over his head for three consecutive fours, then tonked him over square leg for six. The assault continued. Buddha shuffled his attack, bringing on Henry V, medium pace, down the hill, and St Augustine, off-spin and floaters, from the pub end. It made no difference; fast, slow, cunning or downright brutal, it was all meat and drink to the insatiable Spaniard.

At 186 for 6 (Torquemada 72 n.o., Goebbels 59 n.o.) Buddha played a card from the bottom of the pack. Whether or not he knew exactly what he was doing isn't clear, but I was inclined to give him the benefit of the doubt. He signalled to the muffled figure of St Francis of Assisi, who had been patrolling the extra-cover boundary.

For a moment the two were deep in conversation. Obviously there was some difference of opinion, but this was settled and St Francis took the ball. He paced out a longish run at the church end and set a highly aggressive field.

St Francis was one of the characters whose disguise I had not pierced, which is hardly surprising. But it was soon obvious that under that voluminous monkish habit lurked a serious cricketer. He placed two slips and *two* gullies and *two* third men!

His first delivery was a medium-paced loosener. Even so, Torquemada did well not to edge it. St Francis collected the ball, walked back to his mark . . . and then did an unforgivable thing. He hitched up his habit round his waist, secured it with his girdle, and thus revealed to all and sundry a pair of spotless whites and equally impeccable cricket boots. Before we could recover our breath he had torn in, whirled his arm, and delivered quite the fastest ball I'd seen all summer. It shattered Torquemada's wicket and sped away into the long grass.

We were speechless. Quite rightly, Torquemada refused to leave his crease. He argued, that (a) by half-removing his costume the bowler was no longer St Francis of Assisi, (b) such an Act of Transformation had offended good taste, and (c) the chap was clearly a professional. Buddha pointed out that Torquemada himself wore cricket boots and, good taste or not, he would have to go. Rumpelstiltskin hurried onto the field to argue his man's case. St Augustine, egged on by Richard the Lionheart, foolishly tried to manhandle our skipper back to the pavilion, which was the cue for the rest of us to give expression to our feelings.

It was a sordid spectacle, something I hope never to see on a cricket field again. All twenty-two players, plus the umpires, congealed into the roughest maul I've ever been a party to. And it wasn't in the least good-natured. The

Venerable Bede deliberately kneed Crippen in the groin, and the monster suffered a savage bite on the instep.

The match of course had to be abandoned, with no conclusion reached. We all changed back into civilian clothes and, with the briefest of farewells, departed to our various homes.

I spent most of Sunday in bed, nursing bruises and reading Abercrombie's *Up the Spey with Bat and Bible*. I deliberately closed my mind to the previous day's events, and it was only months later I was struck by a telling thought. Why do we cricketers wear whites? For what reason do we all appear on the cricket field identically dressed? The answer stared me in the face. To subdue the ego! Cricket releases such powerful forces in us the game would be unplayable unless a common uniform was the rule. One scene is burned into my memory from the battle of Dingewall – J. S. Bach trying to tear the bolt from Frankenstein's monster's neck. I happen to know the man concerned (we've played shuffleboard occasionally), and violence is not his style. But deck him out in the trappings of the world's leading cantata-monger and you've got a barbarian on your hands. Long may white anonymity clothe even our grandest moments on the field.

10

The Beast of Chardley

Cricket draws its devotees from all walks of life. If you were to stroll into a village pub on any weekend in the summer you would see computer software salesmen, master printers, burglars, policemen and undertakers, all clothed in the white, all preoccupied with the match to come. But in my experience the profession least often represented on the field of play is that of the naturalist, the observer of wild things in the wild state, which surprises me. I'd have thought that cricket would have proved irresistible to the dedicated zoologist. Surely a crowded pavilion between innings would supply as much material for zoological study as, say, a termite hill or a pack of hyenas. To illustrate the point I have set out below an account of the curious behaviour of a team of cricketers in central England. Advocates of the territorial principle in animal conduct will observe that the creatures of Chardley behaved very like grey-eyed Canadian dogfish in defence of their territory, though I admit there are trifling differences. The dogfish doesn't quote Tennyson and cricketers don't mate in the depths of Lake Ontario, but those are small details.

Chardley is a small village in the Vale of the Red Horse. One fine Spring day, just after lunch, Doug Peatfield burst into the public bar of the Mechanical Digger, breathless with bad news.

'Down Lark's Meadow,' he blurted. 'Fellers wi' rollers an' that!'

'Rollers!!'

All eyes turned to Doug. Not being hairdressers, the word 'rollers' could only mean one thing: the contraptions used by groundsmen to flatten cricket pitches.

'Rollers in Lark's Meadow!' cried Ted Lusty, the Chardley skipper, who had just popped into the pub in a fit of camaraderie, 'Did you say fellers wi' rollers?'

This dialogue was repeated, more or less word for word, for the next fifteen minutes. Under its cover let us slip away unnoticed.

The scene shifts to Lark's Meadow, Chardley. This flat and unremarkable field had been rough grazing for as long as anyone could remember. In its time it had been owned by several incompetent farmers, by retired ladies with horses and, briefly, by a man who planned a hot-air balloon taxi service between Birmingham and the centre of London. It might have worked, too, if the wind that had blown the contented traveller south-eastwards to London in the morning hadn't continued to blow south-eastwards in the evening, thus depositing the customers in the Low Countries.

The present landlord of Lark's Meadow was George Weatherstone, the proprietor of the Weatherstone Bathroom Furniture Company. The Weatherstone factory was situated at Longwood, a village not far from Chardley. As such it represented a particularly striking act of lunacy by the Department of the Environment, but this is not the place to discuss the merits of building factories where nobody wants them and where the employees have the greatest difficulty reaching them. Our concern here is with one of the side effects of that act of statesmanship.

The Weatherstone employees, keen to win the Queen's

Award for Industry, demanded a sportsground. The idea was immediately vetoed by management, until it was pointed out that a sportsground represented real estate and could be the source of certain fiscal advantages. Thus management instantly vetoed the veto and set about looking for a likely field that might be sold off to a speculative builder if times got hard. Lark's Meadow, only three miles from Longwood, fitted the bill. Not for one moment did it enter the minds of management that it might be tactless to create a cricket ground within hailing distance of another village. For them Chardley was a geographical irrelevance, not a human fact of life.

Lusty, Peatfield and the others assembled in the public the following evening to voice their feeling of outrage, and plan revenge. The outrage part went very well. None of them had ever come across anything as diabolical in their lives before. Old Albert Ditchburn reckoned it was not far short of drinking someone else's beer. Little Danny Pugh likened it to running off with your best friend's wife, but the majority thought it was worse than that. Bob the shepherd recalled the time his best friend *had* run off with his wife. He'd been very cross at the time but now he couldn't remember what either of them were called. For half an hour or so they all tried to remember what Bob's wife had been called, but when they failed they moved on to the business of retaliation. Somebody suggested letting the wind out of the intruder's car tyres, but this didn't seem to fit the bill. On the other hand the proposal to release Farmer Gilkes' ferocious bull on to the field had a whiff of overkill about it. It was finally decided that Ted Lusty would 'think it over'. Lusty was the ideal person because he was known to have a mean streak. If anyone could devise an underhand way of infuriating the Weatherstonites it was Skipper Lusty.

The drama of Lark's Meadow had begun early in March. By May a pitch of sorts had been beaten out of the reluctant land, and nets erected near the road. Soon workmen arrived with an 'instant' pavilion. One moment it wasn't there; three hours later it was, complete with two coats of paint, benches, the lot. The disgruntled Chardleyites watched the activities with mounting indignation.

'Never seen nothing like it,' said Trevor Peatfield, brother of Doug.

'Bloody disgusting,' said Old Albert.

'That's *always* been rough grazing,' added Little Danny Pugh, who believed that repetition of the obvious was the root of good conversation.

'What's young Ted doin'?' demanded Old Albert. 'Thought he was s'posed to be fixin' 'em.'

'P'raps he's waiting for 'em to start,' suggested Trevor. 'You can't stop 'em till they've started, can you?'

'I'd put the bull on 'em,' said Little Danny.

'You're bloody cracked, that's your trouble,' said Old Albert, and they all wandered off to the Mechanical Digger.

Late in May various people turned up in Lark's Meadow dressed in whites. They bowled to each other in the nets and laughed in a carefree sort of way. On the Friday somebody rolled the strip and on the Saturday morning marked out the pitch. Cars began to arrive at lunch time. Two or three of them had the brass face to go into the Digger and order drinks. The locals sat on their chairs as if carved from wood. Adam, behind the bar, served them very, very slowly, and incorrectly, and over-charged. They didn't stay long, and as soon as their backs were turned a babble of irate conversation burst forth.

'Never seen *nothing* like it,' declared Jack Peatfield, brother of Trevor and Doug. The others agreed. In all their lives they'd never encountered behaviour to match it. Then the door swung open and Ted Lusty entered. The rest of them would have directed their abuse at him had it not been for the crafty smile that disfigured the lower part of his visage. The frowns melted away from their faces.

'You fixed 'em, Ted?' enquired Trevor.

'Reckon so,' said Ted. 'Might go down to Lark's Meadow later on, see how she's going.'

It might be asked why Lusty, Peatfield and the rest were not themselves playing cricket that fine summer afternoon. If I knew, I'd tell you; but I suspect they'd hastily cancelled their match in order to concentrate on the more pressing matter. It's rare for such a thing to happen but, if true, goes to underline the degree of rage burning in the Chardley breasts. It's exactly what the Canadian dogfish would have done.

The Digger closed at three-ish by which time most of the Chardley team had moved off in ones and twos in the direction of Lark's Meadow. As they approached it they paused, like Apaches, in the shadow of the trees, reluctant to expose themselves to the enemy's gaze. And what they saw filled their hearts with bile; strangers enjoying a game of cricket within a few hundred yards of their own pitch! But Ted had fixed 'em. He'd told them so and Ted never lied. It was simply a question of sitting down on the grass and waiting.

The match had been in progress for about an hour and a half when Little Danny Pugh, hidden under a hedge, lifted his head and frowned.

'What's that?'

Charlie Peatfield, brother of Trevor, Doug and Jack, said, 'What's what?'

'That!' said Danny. 'Listen.'

Charlie listened. At first he heard nothing, and then, very faintly behind the noise of the cuckoos and the breeze in the grass, he detected a curiously unnatural sound. Even at a great distance it could be heard to contain several different elements. For instance, a sound that could have been made by someone shuffling a pack of corrugated-iron playing cards. Then something like a flock of sheep being tickled. And a deeper note, defying description.

Charlie seized Danny's arm.

'I know what that is,' he hissed, then shook his head. 'Ted's gone too far this time. We shouldn't 'a let him!'

'What is it?' demanded Danny, as the sound grew louder and nastier.

' 'Tis Durkin's lot,' said Charlie.

The colour drained from Danny's face.

'You mean, let loose . . . out in the open!'

'Must be,' said Charlie, tightly.

Down on the cricket field, unaware of the Apaches in the hills, the match was going nicely. Weatherstone Bathroom Furniture were fielding, and doing rather well. The virgin patch was behaving with all the unpredictability of a meadow torn from its normal role in life. The ball rose sharply, or didn't rise at all, without any relationship to length or speed. Two of the visiting batsmen had retired hurt and the rest had only managed so far to scratch together a meagre total. The proprietor, George Weatherstone, stood proudly before the pavilion clutching his lapels and reflecting on his all-round excellence. Here was a man, he told himself, who was not only an industrial lion, not only the designer of the Weatherstone 'Grand Canyon' Hand Basin with Concealed Overflow, but also a sportsman and public benefactor.

Then the sound reached his ears. To begin with he thought it was internal, the first manifestation of mental breakdown brought on by the incompetence of everyone around him. But this cosy thought was swept aside by an irrational fear. Many years before, as an apprentice fitter in a gas works, he had been present when half the plant exploded. That disaster had been preceded by a sound very like the one he now heard.

Similar signs of uneasiness were showing on the players out in the middle. The non-striking batsman lifted his head like a gazelle that scents an approaching predator. Several fielders did likewise. Soon all thirteen players, plus the umpires, had become gazelles. The bowler faltered in his run-up, his concentration disturbed by something indefinable. The batsman strayed from his crease and gazed towards the road.

As the noise increased so did the likelihood that it bore some relationship to music. Second slip, an accountant and amateur pianist, hissed into the ear of first slip, 'It's *Rosamunde*.' First slip, a snooker player, said, 'Can't be. Sounds more like a band.'

Then, a cry of alarm from deep third man who was nearer the road than anyone else. The cause of his concern had just turned the last corner and was now approaching Lark's Meadow. It was like a huge deformed animal armed with metal spines which were scattered at random along its back. It was the Chardley Silver Band.

A word about the band itself might not be out of place here. It had been formed only six months previously, at the behest of the local police. The youth of Chardley had a bad name in the neighbourhood. Taking their cue from their elders they were vicious, sexually irresponsible and arrogant. They removed gnomes from people's gardens with a nervelessness that astounded the authorities. From gnomes they had moved on to dustbin lids, garden gates and ribald articles of clothing on washing lines. A summit conference had been called by the parish council and the local constabulary. A musical sergeant had suggested a solution. 'Give the little devils something violent to do,' he said. 'Form a band. That'll soak up their aggression.'

Anxious villagers had contributed generously to an Instruments Fund, and the village organist, Mr Durkin, had been blackmailed into taking charge of the whole ghastly project. To everyone's astonishment it had worked. Small Japanese motorbikes had been abandoned for euphoniums, and chain-festooned leather jackets for a uniform of puce and mustard. The members of the band met once a week in an isolated barn. They practised from seven till nine. There wasn't a molecule of musical feeling in any of them, but what you've never known you don't miss. They all agreed it was heaps better than gnomes, though villagers who lived less than two miles from the barn had reservations. This then was the dragon, the Ultimate Option, that Skipper Lusty had released from its lair.

The beast moved at a slovenly march along the lane beside Lark's Meadow. Its appearance matched its many-throated cry. Rooks heaved out of trees and fled. In an adjoining field Farmer Gilkes' ferocious bull ran a dry tongue over dry lips. The match stopped. Confronted by the Chardley Silver Band anything would have stopped. Fifteen pairs of eyes, including those of the umpires, gazed in disbelief. Wives and mothers gathered up their little ones and edged towards their cars. Nature held its breath.

The first man to recover his composure was George Weatherstone. Of course, he said to himself, the peasants of the village were trying to show their appreciation. In their own illiterate way they were saying 'thank you' to the sophisticates of the bathroom furniture business. It was not unlike the head hunters of New Guinea bringing unspeakable gifts to the first white explorers. Having made their gesture they would soon go away and the match could continue. Weatherstone raised his hand to breast level and moved it slowly to left and right in the manner of Royalty expressing enthusiasm. One or two sycophants did the same though they didn't know why.

However, the band didn't go away. Like a huge multi-coloured slug it turned in at the gate to the next field. Roaring its indescribable song it meandered up the far side of the dividing hedge, then came to a halt about a dozen yards from the instant pavilion. For a moment the cacophony stopped, allowing the sound of wailing children to be heard. Then at a signal from Mr Durkin, the brain of the monster, it leapt angrily into a selection from *My Fair Lady*.

The cricketers moved numbly from the pitch and gathered around Weatherstone.

'We can't play with that infernal row going on, sir,' bellowed the skipper.

'I realize that,' bawled Weatherstone, 'but we have to be careful we don't offend them. I suggest we have tea.'

It seemed a brilliant idea. Kettles were filled and boiled, sandwiches produced, and everybody sat down.

So did the band. Right in the middle of what might have been 'Get Me to the Church on Time' Durkin flailed his arms and silence swept across Lark's Meadow. For a second everyone thought they'd gone deaf, then nervous smiles began to flicker across faces. The skipper hurried to the proprietor.

'Look, sir, they're having their tea, too. So let's carry on with the cricket while their mouths are full.'

'Good thinking,' said Weatherstone.

Cups were quickly drained and half-eaten sandwiches hidden in shoes. In no time at all all thirteen players, plus the umpires, were back on the green. The bowler, who had been cut off in mid-over, flexed his muscles, gripped the ball and raced in to the wicket. At the crucial moment, legs spread and arm drawn back, he was struck on the auditory nerve as if by a spanner. Half the band had struck up with what was left of 'Get Me to the Church' and the other half with the ballet music from *Faust*, the next piece in their programme. The bowler stumbled and fell, the batsman reared away and the rest of the players fled from the field.

George Weatherstone was a bad loser. But he wasn't a complete fool either. Obviously the peasants had misunderstood the signals. He had been too tactful, which can be a mistake with simple people. Finding a gap in the hedge he made his way to the cause of the trouble. The band had stopped as soon as the players had left the field and the members were now seated, eating hunks of bread and jam and playfully hitting each other with their instruments. Weatherstone approached Durkin, smiling warmly.

'Delightful,' he said, 'quite delightful. However, I wonder if you would be kind enough not to play while the match is in progress. It's a bit distracting for the cricketers.'

Durkin, who had been railroaded into the job in the first place and had since been threatened with violence by Ted Lusty, smiled benignly.

'Thank you very much,' he said. 'There are unmistakable signs of improvement, aren't there?'

'Unmistakable,' said Weatherstone, 'but you won't start up while we're playing, will you?'

'*My Fair Lady*', said Durkin. 'That's next. We've done a lot of work on that.'

Only then did it occur to Weatherstone that Durkin was deaf. This was a recent handicap, going back no further than the inauguration of the band. It was a slight hindrance to his organ playing but none at all to his conducting.

Weatherstone, foiled again, turned angrily to the nearest uniformed lout who happened to be thrusting his cornet up the trouser leg of a bass trombone.

'You!' he snapped. 'Tell your troop of baboons I want *no* music, do you understand? One more peep and I shall call the police.'

The speed of his exit denied him the sight of the cornet appearing above the waistband of the trombonist's trousers, but he was satisfied he'd solved the problem. It was what he was good at.

It was decided to finish tea, so it was another twenty minutes before the refreshed cricketers re-assembled on the pitch. The bowler still had three balls to bowl, and he returned to his mark full of optimism. The band was still sprawled on the grass, fighting and screaming. The animal had returned to its jelloid, unicellular state. Again the bowler gripped the ball, flexed his muscles and ran up to the wicket. It was probably the sound of leather on willow that did the damage. It seemed to have the same effect on the band as the ringing of bells on Pavlov's dogs. The fighting stopped instantly, they all leapt to their feet, seized their instruments and blew. Music written by a number of different composers billowed into the air like debris from a volcano. Again the rooks heaved out of the trees.

The thirteen cricketers, plus the umpires and George Weatherstone, turned, and as one man charged for the gap in the hedge, fists raised in anger. The musicians saw them coming and began to edge away, as musicians will when attacked by cricketers. It was like a scene from Eisenstein's *Alexander Nevsky*, though with a smaller cast. Soon the Whites were in amongst the Puce and Mustards, bats clattering with Wagner tubas.

Most people would have put their money on the Chardley Silver Band in a free-for-all of this sort, made up as it was of hardened criminals. But the cricketers were fighting for a principle – the rights of conquest – and there is no question they would have won the day had it not been for the appearance of the Apaches. Suddenly out of the trees raced Lusty, Pugh and innumerable Peatfields, fists bunched. The cricketers paused, then turned and fled. Cars were started, bags and socks flung into boots. Soon Lark's Meadow was cleared of the last invader. Only the instant pavilion remained, but as Ginger Peatfield remarked, 'Thou shalt hear the "Never, never", whispered by the phantom years', which seemed to hit the nail on the head.

11

Out of the Deep

It's an odd thing that although the Royal Navy has produced a number of excellent cricketers almost none of them have come from the submarine service. I've heard it said that this is because sailors find it fiddly erecting a proper net in a submarine, particularly when submerged, but I can't accept that. One of the best extra covers I ever knew was raised in a lighthouse, which seems to answer that objection.

There was, however, one heroic exception to this puzzling state of affairs and it involved not just one submariner, but a whole team. None were good cricketers in the sense you and I understand the term, but they knew the rudiments. And, above all, they had guts. Their story is not to be found in W. S. Churchill's *The Gathering Storm*, nor in Hesketh's *Afloat with Bat and Ball*. I came across it in a book of rum tales for children, whence I have rescued it for a nobler posterity. These men, I believe, deserve better than to be bracketed with whistling fish and the largest pygmy in the world.

It was Summer, 1939. His Majesty's Submarine *Bloater* was stationed in the eastern Pacific. The news from Europe wasn't good. There had been disturbances outside Lord's Tavern, and some agent provocateur had scrawled the words 'Bolshevik Agitator' across a photograph of Ranjitsinhji and sent it to the French ambassador. The Captain and crew of *Bloater* were very much on their toes, particularly as luxury liners, crammed with lederhosen-clad Aryans, had been reported off the coast of Ecuador.

The skipper of *Bloater* was Lieutenant-Commander 'Nipper' Gladworth, son of Uriah Gladworth, the Yorkshire romantic. 'Nipper' loved engines; always had. His greatest pleasure in life was to strip off his coat and plunge his arms into sump oil. He would spend many off-duty hours just pottering about in the engine room, his ear cocked for promising noises. One may imagine his panic-stricken delight, therefore, when he was roused from his bunk by the chief engineer with the news that the crown sprocket had thrown a tooth, that thrust was down by seventy two per cent and consumption rampant.

Even before the skipper had plunged his arms into the sump – which he did nevertheless – it was obvious they would have to put into port pretty smartly. If word reached the luxury liners that the R.N. was in trouble, there could be far-reaching consequences. The news would be flashed to Berlin. Buttons would be pressed. Hundreds of fair-haired tourists all over the world would rip off their lederhosen to reveal beneath them the uniforms of Colonels of the Panzer Grenadier. Gladworth had to move fast, yet deviously.

The nearest port was Valparaiso. The chief engineer was sure he could find the means to repair the damage there. Shouldn't take more than a few hours, he opined. But of course they'd have to make damn sure no word leaked out to the natives. As we all know, the Chileans are a delightful race of people – handsome and intelligent, but, at that moment in history, neutral. Also, heavily infiltrated by blond tourists. If it became the common talk of the water-front that *Bloater* was out of action, a squadron of German pocket battleships would immediately appear, ensuring the loss of the whole of South America to the cause of democracy.

To start with all went well. *Bloater* put in under cover of darkness and the chief engineer soon had the damaged engine in bits all over the floor. In the morning Gladworth paid courtesy visits to the British Legation, the Valparaiso Polo Club, and the local branch of Marks & Spencer. He returned after lunch, expecting to find his vessel ready for sea. He was in for a shock.

'It's worse than we thought,' said the chief engineer. 'The lower dredge pins are shot to ribbons and the gawping valve simply won't close. It's going to take a couple of days at least.'

'Great Harry!' cried 'Nipper'. 'We'll be the talk of the *Unter den Linden*!'

'Unless we can think of a wheeze,' said Sub-Lieutenant Palfry, the ship's intellectual. 'If we can pretend we're here for some other reason nobody will pay any attention to us.'

'*What* other reason!' snapped 'Nipper'.

'Well . . . how about a whist drive? Or a musical evening?'

Then up spoke the Chief Petty Officer.

'How about a cricket match, sir? It'll take the natives at least a week to get a team together, by which time we can be up and away.'

Gladworth fixed the CPO with a steely glance.

'By God, that's brilliant! Palfry, go ashore immediately and fix it up. And don't rush.'

Palfry didn't rush. It wasn't his style. He spent two hours window-shopping and another twenty minutes negotiating the purchase of a lawn mower. Then he made his first mistake. As he spoke no Spanish, he went to Marks &

Spencer to raise the matter of the cricket match. The local manager, a man called Niblett, was extremely helpful, which is hardly surprising considering that his uncle had had a trial for Norfolk.

Palfry was a little taken aback.

'You'll probably need a few days to get a side together, won't you?' he said.

'Absolutely not,' said Niblett. 'We've got plenty of chaps desperate for a game.'

'You mean, you've got a pitch and gear, and all that?'

'We're the best equipped club in South America,' said Niblett, without a hint of vanity.

Palfry snatched at a passing straw.

'Ah, yes, but we want to play against Chileans,' he said, 'not just Englishmen.'

'Most of them are Chileans,' said Niblett, 'and damn good, too. Shall we say eleven o'clock, tomorrow morning?'

'But look here,' said the unhappy Palfry, 'won't you want to cut the grass, and things?'

'My dear Mr Palfry,' said the local manager, 'by eleven o'clock tomorrow morning not only will we have a pitch, rolled and marked, and a team, and umpires and scorers, we shall probably have about two hundred spectators as well. Everybody loves the Navy. This is going to be quite an occasion.'

'Nipper' Gladworth was furious, but mostly with himself. One should never send a boy to do a man's work. His first thought was to make Palfry skipper of the team, to teach him a lesson, but that would only have compounded the error. It had to be someone with a knowledge of life, and deeply devious. One candidate stood head and shoulders above the others.

'Chief Petty Officer,' said 'Nipper', 'I want you to pick

a team, get out there tomorrow at eleven o'clock, and stay out there. I don't want to see any of you for forty-eight hours. Is that clear?'

'Aye aye, sir,' said the CPO.

Chief Petty Officer Groath was a short, stoutish man, as are all chief petty officers. He was not a particularly distinguished sailor, and even less of a cricketer, but he did have a profound knowledge of human nature. He knew, for instance, that orders mattered more than morals or common sense. If the skipper wanted a cover for forty-eight hours then a cover for forty-eight hours he would have. If it meant manipulating the laws of man and God, then manipulated they would be.

He suffered his first disappointment almost immediately. There was only one member of the crew who had ever played cricket at a decent level before. This was the chief engineer, but of course he was not available for selection. There were two Able Seamen who claimed to have played a 'bit of cricket' but Groath ruled them out on the grounds that anyone who volunteered for anything without having had his fingers stamped on had to have to have some villainous motive.

The final eleven didn't look particularly promising. They were all 'pressed' men, even the officers. Several had never even seen the game played. Leading Seaman O'Callaghan, a boxer of some ability, appealed against his selection on the grounds that he might suffer a mutilating injury. But Gladworth was unmoved.

The ground of the East Pacific Cricket and Country Club was situated at a delightful spot called San Cristobal, a little way inland. A large white club house built on the lines of Raffles Hotel in Singapore overlooked the most perfect cricket ground any of the submariners had ever seen. True, some of them had never seen any sort of cricket ground, but that doesn't alter the fact that this was an absolute archbishop of a pitch.

The *Bloater* XI was conveyed from Valparaiso in an old Albion bus. When they arrived at San Cristobal, they were shocked to find the place a-buzz with activity. Handsome ladies and gentlemen, obviously the cream of local society, strolled hither and thither around the ground eagerly discussing the match. As the bus jerked to a halt outside the club house, a small crowd of spectators pushed elegantly forward. Hats were raised and a splatter of applause broke out as Groath and his team mates clambered out.

Niblett hurried down the steps and seized the hand of the leading seaman who, of course, was the Chief Petty Officer.

'Welcome to the East Pacific,' he said warmly. 'Would you like someone to pick up your baggage?'

Baggage!

'Er . . .,' began the Chief Petty Officer, for whom the word baggage meant something different.

Sub Lieutenant Palfry elbowed his way forward.

'Matter of fact, we haven't got any,' he said. 'We were wondering if you would be good enough to tog us out?'

'You haven't got anything?' enquired the surprised Niblett. 'Not even whites?'

'Nothing,' said Palfry. 'Had to throw all our cricket gear over the side. A hurricane off the Horn. Everything had to go – bats, gloves, my stamp collection, the lot.'

'How ghastly,' said Niblett. 'But please don't give it another thought. We can provide everything you need. Meanwhile, the President would be delighted if you'd join him in something to lay the dust.'

'That would be much appreciated,' said Groath, who had instantly assumed his rightful position at the front of the team. 'Caps off, lads, and . . .', lowering his voice, '. . .

mind yer manners. No, sir, not you,' he said quickly to Lieutenant Bird, the senior officer present. 'I was addressing the lower deck.'

Drinks were taken in the President's Dining Room. Everybody, regardless of rank, age or susceptibility, ordered large whiskies and sodas. Only Able Seaman Onslow had the glass wrenched discreetly from his fingers.

'No you don't, me lad,' whispered the all-knowing and unforgiving Groath. 'We haven't forgotten what happened at Trincomalee have we? It's fruit cup, or nothing!'

Suitably refreshed, the *Bloater* XI were shown to their dressing-room, which was Roman Colonial in style. A quantity of crisp whites, shirts, socks and boots had been laid out for their inspection. Lieutenant Bird, the senior officer present, had first pick, then Sub-Lieutenant Palfry, and so on down to Able Seaman Onslow – who, unlike the rest, was awash with fruit cup and in a mood to find fault.

'Leave the two top buttons undone, and you'll be all right,' said Groath. 'Just don't bend down, that's all.'

So they came to the question of the batting order.

Cricket in the Services leaves no room for debate or second thoughts in the matter of batting order. One goes in strictly according to rank. Thus a sixty-year-old Admiral would always precede a younger, fitter Vice-Admiral, and an ex-England opener who happened to be an Able Seaman would always go in last. The Chief Petty Officer knew the rules and it took him no time at all to complete the card:

Lieutenant Bird
Sub-Lieutenant Palfry
Midshipman Meadowfield
Chief Petty Officer Groath
Petty Officer Gentle
Leading Seaman O'Callaghan

Artificer Staunch
Able Seaman Lithgow-Hughes
Able Seaman Seaman
Able Seaman Mussorgsky
Able Seaman Onslow

Even before the transformation from jolly sailormen to gentlemen cricketers had been completed a native messenger arrived at the door of the visitor's dressing room with a note. The Captain of the East Pacific XI presented his compliments and cordially invited the Captain of the *Bloater* XI to join him in the middle for the toss.

'If you win,' said Bird, 'put them in. With any luck we can have them batting all day. Don't forget, we've got to keep this farce up until tomorrow evening.'

The East Pacific skipper was an Anglo-Hungarian mining engineer called Dohnanyi. He came from a long line of dashing cavalry officers and was not impressed by sailors, and certainly not by Chief Petty Officer Groath. He spun. Groath called tails, and tails it was.

'Ah, so you'll be batting,' said the mining engineer.

'That's where you're wrong, my son,' said Groath who had noted the contemptuous look in the eye of his opposite number, and hadn't cared for it. 'You're batting. We're doing the other bit.'

The next problem was picking a wicketkeeper. Bird said it had to be someone who knew what he was doing, which wasn't helpful. Meadowfield volunteered, but was ruled out on account of his youth. Petty Officer Gentle said he'd seen it done and was prepared to have a go. But in the end the choice fell on Artificer Staunch, because he was clever with his hands. Bird said he would open the bowling from the pepper trees end, and that Palfry would take the other end. It's not usual for the bowling to be allocated on the basis of rank, as is batting, because, unlike batting, bowling is considered to be manual labour and can be left to the socially less-fortunate. But on this occasion Bird felt that the likes of Mussorgsky and Onslow weren't to be trusted, a view heartily endorsed by skipper Groath.

The East Pacific openers were young, fit, slim and obviously heirs to great wealth. Groath hated them on sight, which may explain why he set such an eccentric field. He placed his men in a circle around the facing batsman, allowing a small gap on the strip itself through which the bowled ball might pass. The opener in question, a young clergyman from Worcester making his first trip abroad, was alarmed by the tactic and peered anxiously between Gentle at silly mid-on and Lithgow-Hughes at silly mid-off for a sight of the bowler. Bird's problem was not dissimilar which may have accounted for his first delivery being less than dead straight. It struck Lithgow-Hughes a glancing blow on the temple and sped away to third man.

'*Si-i-i* . . !' yelled the clergyman's partner.

Able Seaman Seaman was the man nearest to the ball and he wondered if he should run after it. Groath invited him to do so, as did Bird, Palfry and a few others, so he did. He threw it back in the general direction of his shipmates. Onslow, a largish man, leapt to catch it and in the process staggered into the non-striking batsman, who was on his third run. Both men crashed to the ground and the ball ran loose. Able Seaman Mussorgsky snatched it up and threw it towards the senior officer present, hoping to curry favour. It missed Bird but struck Leading Seaman O'Callaghan in the back and ricocheted into the stumps. As luck would have it the clergyman from Worcester had made his ground but, seeing the heap of bodies lying in the middle of the pitch, felt he should get back to the other end. As he raced passed the carnage Onslow, who was an integral part of it, stuck out a leg. The clergyman crashed heavily. Meadowfield, in a state of near hysteria at all the excitement, picked up the ball and threw it to wicketkeeper Artificer Staunch. It was a marvellous throw. It was nowhere near Staunch but it did remove the middle stump. The square leg umpire raised his finger. The clergyman got unsteadily to his feet and limped off to the Club House.

Chief Petty Officer Groath reviewed the situation. One of the enemy eliminated and another seriously damaged (Onslow's victim was having difficulty getting to his feet). On the debit side Lithgow-Hughes had a largish gash on the side of his head, which he probably wouldn't notice till later. But the skipper was now approached by an agitated Lieutenant Bird.

'This is disastrous,' said the senior bowler present. 'If we go on like this, the match will be over before lunch. We *mustn't* get them out, Chief Petty Officer.'

'Aye aye, sir,' said the skipper.

In Groath's opinion the villain of the piece was Able Seaman Onslow. He had been involved in both acts of violence and, if not deterred, would go through the opposition like grape shot. He approached the evil-doer menacingly.

'Have you no idea of how to behave on a cricket pitch, Onslow?'

Onslow looked confused.

'I didn't mean to tread on him,' he said. 'I just stepped back and there he was.'

'You're a disgrace to the Royal Navy, Onslow. I shouldn't be surprised if your name isn't brought to the attention of the First Sea Lord.'

'Sorry, Chief.'

'I want you out of the firing line, son. We can't afford another debarkle. I want you to go and stand down there, where them funny bushes are. And stay there. If that little red ball comes anywhere near you, ignore the bloody thing. Am I making myself clear?'

'Yes, Chief.'

'Right. Double away.'

During this exchange of views the next batsman had arrived at the crease. It was Dohnanyi, the skipper. His natural contempt for the sea and everything connected with it had now turned to blind rage. He took guard with a menacing expression and glared at the ring of fielders. They all edged back a few inches. Bird bowled. The ball was wide, but not beyond the reach of a man who came from a long line of cavalry officers. It flew from his bat like an armour-piercing shell and struck the Chief Petty Officer, fielding at forward point, just above the fly buttons. Groath gasped, and clutched his stomach. A horrified silence fell across the ground. Surely no-one, not even a Chief Petty Officer, could withstand such a murderous blow. All eyes were on him as he slowly straightened his back, quietly uttering some nautical remark as he did so. He then raised his hand slowly in the air. Clutched in it was the ball. Midshipman Meadowfield, trembling at first slip, muttered 'How's that?' between dried lips, and the umpire raised his finger.

Groath made his way sheepishly to Lieutenant Bird.

'It was done in self defence, sir,' he said. 'If I could have ducked, I'd have ducked.'

'Not your fault,' said Bird tersely. 'Though you didn't have to hang on to the wretched thing.'

'Matter of fact, I thought it was one of my internal organs,' explained the Chief. 'If I'd known what it was . . .'

'All right, all right,' said Bird, 'but we're going to have to pull our socks up. Put everybody on the boundary, and give instructions that the ball is not to be interfered with in any way. Carry on, Chief Petty Officer.'

In cricketing terms this tactic leaves something to be desired, but from the point of view of national security it was entirely successful. The home batsmen found that not only was it possible to score two or three runs from even the most insipid shot, but boundaries, too, were simply there for the hitting. The ball would pass within inches of unmoving fielders, sometimes even between their legs, and by lunch time the score had moved from 2 for 2 to 117 for 2. Tea was taken at ten past four with the scoreboard showing 306 for 2. Talk of declaration was in the air but Dohnanyi would have none of it. His proud Anglo-Magyar blood still bubbled with hatred. Niblett murmured something about leaving enough time to get 'them' out, at which Dohnanyi simply laughed. The East Pacific attack, of which he was the spearhead, would go through them like hussars through custard, as he colourfully put it.

At ten to six, the Andes ablaze with pink light from the declining sun, the score stood at 389 for 2. The *Bloater* XI were grey with exhaustion. Bird, Palfry and Meadowfield had bowled over ninety overs between them, and several of the fielders were privately wondering if perhaps world war would not have been a preferrable option.

Dohnanyi then declared. The jolly jacks crept from the field like blobs of lard and melted onto the floor of their dressing-room. Able Seaman Seaman expressed a common feeling when he muttered 'If I could only get my hands on that ruddy Adolph Hitler . . !' But after a shower and glass of refreshing passion fruit juice (only half a glass for Onslow), they all felt a little brighter. The senior officer present outlined the position.

'It's like this,' said Bird. 'We've got to bat from now until six o'clock tomorrow evening. Luckily the opposition has played into our hands. It's unlikely that we shall score the required three hundred and ninety runs before stumps, which should give them enough time back at *Bloater*.'

Artificer Staunch, who had only conceded fifty-nine byes all afternoon, begged leave to make a point.

'But it's not so much the runs, is it, sir? As I see it, it's more like not getting out.'

'I was coming to that,' said Bird. 'The object of the exercise is survival, and for those who haven't played a lot of cricket I'd like to give you a few tips that may come in useful. One, no fancy shots. If the ball's straight stick your leg down the wicket and just let it hit you. It hardly hurts at all. Two, if the ball's not straight leave the damn thing alone. Three, never attempt a run. Any man who leaves his crease will be fined a week's pay. Right-ho, Mr Palfry, let's get padded up.'

The spirit of Trafalgar was not shamed that late Chilean afternoon. Bird and Palfry made their unhurried way to the wicket like men strolling along the Macao water-front. But in fact both were desperately preoccupied. Bird was worried about Meadowfield, who looked as if he might crack under the pressure. Palfry was worried about the ball, which, so he had heard, could inflict terrible injuries.

The first over was to be bowled by the skipper, Dohnanyi. Bird was glad about this. Better that he should face the full force of this storm rather than someone lower down the order. He dreaded to think what the likes of Mussorgsky or Able Seaman Seaman would have done in a similar position.

Dohnanyi disappeared into the distance, then reappeared travelling at an unbelievable speed. The ball flew from his hand and Bird lunged forward to meet it. Even before he'd completed his stroke the sound of whirring bails filled the air, plus cries of 'Olé!' from the direction of the Club House. Bird went cold. What now lay between the British

Empire and the Fascist menace? Meadowfield, Chief Petty Officer Groath, and Onslow. As he made his way back to the dressing-room Bird wondered how long it would be before word reached the Admiralty. With luck war would break out first.

Bird hardly dared to watch as Meadowfield strode, almost ran, to the wicket, his brave unshaven cheeks pink with valour. And he unashamedly closed his eyes as the midshipman launched himself at Dohnanyi's next delivery. The ball went for four. The next ball was flung down at even greater speed. Meadowfield missed it. So did the wicketkeeper. Palfry, reacting to an instinct older than the sea itself, shouted 'Come one!' and they came one. Palfry immediately regretted his lack of control. The expression on the bowler's face would have cut the rust from a ship's bottom. He never saw the ball, merely felt the bat twitch in his hand, and heard the cries of ' 'Zat?!' as the keeper scooped up the catch.

Chief Petty Officer Groath survived two deliveries by simply allowing the ball to strike him about the body. The third ball was a yorker. His person was thinner at the lower end and the middle stump cartwheeled fifty yards.

Meadowfield played the next over cautiously, but he couldn't get the single run that would have taken him to the striker's end for the next over. Petty Officer Gentle claimed he wasn't ready after being caught at first slip, and Leading Seaman O'Callaghan simply backed away. For a man who had cut down innumerable opponents in the ring he was curiously diffident at the wicket.

At least Staunch and Lithgow-Hughes tried. Both were bowled for nought, middle stump, but they'd obeyed orders. No fancy strokes or cheeky singles; just the front leg down the wicket and the bat well out of harm's way. Able Seaman Seaman hit a six. In fact he'd been trying to protect himself from a bouncer, and the ball had carried over the boundary. Led astray by the applause that followed this shot, he tried it again, but this time the ball was in a different place.

Able Seaman Mussorgsky was stumped, which had the merit of originality. He ambled forward to play the ball, missed it, and was astonished to find himself given out. He would have asked for clarification, but everyone, even Meadowfield, seemed agreed on the decision.

Thus it was that the last batsman, Able Seaman Onslow, arrived at the wicket. Onslow was one of those people who's not terribly good at anything. He couldn't knit, or play the violin, and he was incapable of dividing by nine. He was, in fact, a man with nothing to lose. If he got out for a duck, first ball, at least he'd be doing no worse than the senior officer present. And if he lasted for two balls, or got a run, he'd have overtaken the best the ward room had to offer. And so Onslow, who promised little and delivered less, decided to get his head down.

To describe his performance as dogged would be to misuse the language. This was heroism and application far beyond the call of duty. He played and missed five balls out of six. He was dropped twice. And then, to his astonishment, he got one in the middle of the bat. In some mysterious way this seemed to unlock a door that had remained shut fast all his life. It suddenly occurred to him that he was good at something. He was good at hitting a cricket ball. So he hit it again. And again. The field spread. The bowling became erratic. The harder he hit the ball the more the opposition wilted. It was easy.

Able Seaman Onslow was just two runs off his fifty when, unknown to him, Lieutenant Bird was called to the telephone. It was 'Nipper' Gladworth.

'We've fixed it,' said the breathless skipper. 'We'll be

ready to sail in an hour. Get back here straight away.'

'Aye aye, sir,' said the delighted Bird. 'We're on our way.'

Suddenly it was all over. Suddenly there was the Lieutenant on the boundary waving his arms and shouting.

'Come on, you two, we've declared. The game's finished.'

'But we haven't won yet,' said Meadowfield.

'Don't argue!' bellowed Bird angrily.

On the bus journey back to Valparaiso it was noticeable that no-one over the rank of Leading Seaman talked to Onslow. O'Callaghan and Mussorgsky said they thought he'd done terribly well, and Able Seaman Seaman thought Onslow should take it up as a living. Onslow liked that. It was nice to be appreciated by your shipmates. And it was nice to be ignored by the three stiffnecks at the front of the bus. True, Midshipman Meadowfield had said 'Jolly good show,' when no-one was listening, but he hadn't grown up to be a proper officer yet. Obviously the other two were furious, and that was nice.

So *Bloater* slipped out on the evening tide and was soon lost to view among the heaving grey mountains of the Pacific Ocean. But she left behind her a legend. One day eleven ruffians had emerged from the depths of the sea, played the most barbaric game of cricket anyone had ever seen, then mysteriously disappeared. Why? There was no rhyme or reason to it.

Visitors to the East Pacific Cricket and Country Club still wonder at the sailor's cap that hangs behind the bar, adorned with the faded letters 'H. M. Submarine'. Apparently, it was accidently left behind in the rush for the bus that summer long ago. By Onslow, of course.

12

Only the Match was Lost

Although the Laws of Cricket are not as old as the Ten Commandments and were revealed to the world in a less theatrical manner, they are, nevertheless, rather more effective than their Middle Eastern equivalents. For instance, folk have been coveting their neighbour's ass, wife, washing-machine, etc. for donkey's years without ever receiving a curt note from headquarters, but if an umpire were to allow a player to use a bat wider than four and a half inches he would be unfrocked within the week. Bearing false witness is particularly rampant in the world, even in the Cotswolds, but fielding the ball with an article of one's clothing is virtually unknown.

It may be thought that Moses' set suffers from overcomplication and rigidness, but our Laws are no less detailed. Take the lbw situation, for instance; or, if you'd rather not, consider the question of bad light. Moses would have needed a barrow-load of tablets to accommodate the revealed truth on that one subject alone. And runners. There is nothing in the Commandments remotely approaching the labyrinthine matter of batsmen's runners. So convoluted is it that I have known matches stopped or abandoned, because the umpires and captains couldn't agree. One match in particular is tattooed on my memory. It was Fuzzel Mallet *v.* the Bar Flies. I wasn't a regular with the Flies, but their usual off-spinner was still damp from an earlier fixture and I was asked to take his place.

Fuzzel lies on the edge of Exmoor, a place where occasionally fielders are trampled by stags. It is also a favourite watering hole of the Bar Flies. They arrive on Friday night, drink until all signs of life are eliminated, then take the field next afternoon like men cut out of tissue paper. Two questions will immediately suggest themselves. How do these wraiths manage to get through a game of cricket? And how did I, a moderate in all things, ever come to get involved with them? The answer to the first is fairly simple. Good coaching in early life and a total insensitivity to pain, risk, and the jibes of the spectators. The second question still baffles me.

In this particular match Fuzzel Mallet won the toss and chose to bat. Our fast bowler broke down after two deliveries and had to be treated with ice cubes, which was a pity because we really had nobody else. Our second line of attack was armed with pig's bladders rather than howitzers, and the Fuzzel batsmen simply queued up to hit boundaries. As usual, I didn't get on until the cause was lost. It's not surprising I didn't get a wicket. The batsmen were so intoxicated with confidence they simply ignored the subtleties of my off-spin. A good bowler needs a good batsman to show him at his best, not gorillas with clubs.

The Fuzzel Mallet total was 210. It would have been a great deal more if the home side had been fitter. It takes energy to keep on hitting the ball, however inviting the delivery, and our hosts were not long on energy. They, too, had celebrated the night before, but lacked our years of training.

If the first innings was a tasteless charade, our second was nothing less than a disgrace, not only to good fellowship and decency, but to cricket itself. Of our first four batsmen two were declared incapable, one genuinely ill, and the fourth ruled out owing to the loss of his Bar Flies cap without which he childishly refused to go to the wicket. Thus two men who should have been resting in a darkened room tottered out to open our reply.

Hoskins was about forty and had once been a fair bat. His partner, Flood, was younger but less sound. On this occasion both had eyes like keyholes, so perhaps it is irrelevant to mention such things as age and ability. The first ball Hoskins faced was a wide, which was fortunate because at the moment the bowler brought over his arm Hoskins saw a mauve beaver in the middle of the pitch. The next was a little straighter. The third delivery was short and fast, and dead on the middle stump. Hoskins' response was a thing of beauty, a stroke straight out of the coaching manual, though not for that particular delivery. It struck him between the eyes with a wooden 'clunk'. Hoskins seemed quite unaware of what had happened. Fielders ran forward anxiously, only to be met by a look of mild surprise from the batsman. The game resumed.

Flood, a vet, was having a thinnish time at the other end. I suspect he was seeing several balls at the same time and unfailingly chose the wrong one to play. He did get four lucky leg-byes off his ankle, and a streaky two off the side of his face, but overall it wasn't a convincing performance. But soon attention was diverted away from him. In the middle of the fifth over Hoskins, the non-striker, quietly collapsed. As the bowler returned to his mark our chief hope elegantly altered his position from the vertical to the horizontal, without either dislodging his cap or the smile on his face. He was carried from the field, cold as a duck, and was not seen up and about again for several days.

Parsons now walked to the crease. I've always liked Parsons. He's a civilized, quietly-spoken man. Even plundered by drink he will continue to talk engagingly about dry stone walling, whether anyone's there or not. But this amiability conceals a Shakespearean thirst, and I feared for him on this occasion.

My fear was not misplaced. The second ball struck Parsons a sickening blow on the foot. Any normal man would have given a cry of anguish, flung down his bat and tugged at his boot laces. Not Parsons. He simply squared up for the next delivery. It was down the leg side, requiring a slight adjustment of the feet. As he attempted to make this adjustment some anatomical function objected. The injured foot refused to obey orders from HQ and Parsons measured his length on the pitch. The prone figure was immediately surrounded by fielders. Colleagues made ready to move him to the pavilion, but Parsons would have none of it. He rose slowly to his feet and gazed at no one in particular.

'Sorry,' he said. 'I shall require a runner. Foot won't work. Awfully sorry.'

Bellflower, our number eleven, volunteered. He was the best singer in the team. Cricket was more or less a closed book to him, but his voice was loud and his memory prodigious. His version of 'My Mother Bids Me Bind My Hair' has secured us many fixtures that might otherwise have been lost. But his knowledge of the Laws was skimpy, and this worried some of us. There was no question that he would run and run; the problem was, where to, and at whose bidding?

Bellflower took up his post at square leg and instantly dropped into the attitude of a sprinter. The bowler, a humanitarian, bowled a gentle long-hop. It would seem that Parsons nearly saw it, since it hit his bat and trickled towards first slip. Some oaf in the pavilion shouted 'Run', so Bellflower ran. The wicketkeeper gathered the ball and threw down the stumps. Bellflower was now somewhere in the region of mid-wicket. The umpire signalled 'out' and our skipper, Jingo Harrison, hurried on to the field shaking his fist.

'You can't stump a runner!' he bellowed.

The umpire, a tall, dark-visaged man – a descendant of the last village hangman, so I was told – glared dangerously.

'Get that 'ooligan off the field!' he growled.

Harrison is one of those people in whom the milk of human kindness runs thin. I've even known him argue crossly with small children about Father Christmas's exact address, so you may imagine his reaction to the hangman's brusque words.

'If you don't understand the ruddy Laws you shouldn't be ruddy umpiring!'

The hangman closed in on him.

'I didn't give 'im out stumped. He were run out. Now, git off!'

This exchange of views highlights, in a somewhat rustic way, one of the most trying problems facing the law-giver. Namely, the interpretation of the facts. The Laws themselves are clear-cut; life is not, particularly on the cricket field. The Book may be unequivocal about who is or is not stumped, but is blank when it comes to human muddle. The umpire is the sole judge, and umpires are susceptible to error, pressure, incompetence, bribery and motes of dust in the eye.

Jingo Harrison knew all about error and was in no doubt that Parsons was its victim. Likewise Culpepper, the Fuzzel Mallet captain. Maybe it was compassion – we were 10 for 5 at the time – or simply that the pub didn't open for another two and a half hours. Either way, he drew the hangman to one side and persuaded him that from where he was standing it did look a bit like a stumping. The hangman, clearly piqued, glared into space.

'Not out,' he muttered darkly, 'despite all evidence to the cont'ry.'

Jingo had a brief baleful word with Bellflower, then left the field. Again play was resumed.

For about eight minutes nothing exciting happened, then Parsons hit a four. Bellflower set off for a run, Parsons called him back. Flood called him a rude name, and the ball, returned at speed from the boundary, struck Flood behind the left knee. His slow descent to the ground was straight out of the Royal Ballet's repertoire. Again a prone figure was surrounded by fielders, colleagues, dogs, wives and umpires. Several people made a fireman's chair on to which Flood was placed. Then Jingo Harrison arrived, elbowing his way through the crowd.

'Put that man down!' he ordered.

Flood, wracked with the sort of pain that makes men denounce their grandmothers to the secret police, was lowered on to his one sound leg.

'You!' snapped Jingo, pointing at Horace Blumenthal. 'Runner.'

Horace was our fast bowler, the one who had broken down after two whirls of the arm.

'But, Jingo . . .' he blurted.

'Shut up. Parsons is just getting into his stride. Every man's got to bat till he's out, cricket-fashion. Let's get on with it!

What followed was barely watchable. Our two batsmen, Parsons and Flood, were each reduced to standing on one leg. Blumenthal had severe ringing in the ears, and Bellflower, though fit physically, was intellectually out of his depth. The Fuzzel bowlers were as dismayed as the rest of us. How slowly and how wide may one bowl to a man who has blood oozing from his boot? They did their best for us, poor devils, but only minutes later Parsons crashed across his stumps and had to be given out 'hit wicket', which was an understatement. He was carried back to the pavilion to sympathetic applause.

Jingo Harrison himself now strode to the wicket. At last, a player with a relatively clear head and a gutful of determination. The field spread. The bowler licked his fingers. The ball carved its way through the summer air, nipped passed Jingo's forward lunge, and took out the middle stump.

The silence that followed would have done credit to a catacomb, and none was more silent than Harrison himself. I swear that at the moment leather struck ash the skipper would have taken on all the pains and disasters of his team mates just for one more chance. I think even the home side would have been prepared to make an exception in his case, but the stump sagged and the bails were grounded. Only a no-ball could have saved him, but the umpire at the bowler's end came from a long line of executioners. Jingo Harrison left the crease a broken reed, a spent shot, with a W. in the bowler's box and an egg in his own.

It was now Blumenthal's turn to bat. Although nominally performing as Flood's runner it was clear he was going to need a runner himself. It should have been the skipper, but he had disappeared into the trees behind the pavilion. There was only one person left. Me.

Perhaps I should update the reader on the state of play. We were 7 wickets down for 12. In all their history the Bar Flies had never been dismissed for under 25. Honour and tradition were at stake. Flood, incredibly, was still at the wicket. His runner had been Blumenthal, but Blumenthal was now his partner, and I had become Blumenthal's runner. Readers may wonder what had happened to Bellflower. He had left the field when Parsons collapsed but now returned to become Flood's runner. So we had Flood (Bellflower) and Blumenthal (me).

Although we didn't know it at the time, Horace Blumenthal was now near the apex of his nervous breakdown, or personality change, call it what you like. But he had just enough of his wits left to realize he had to get to the non-striker's end and stay there. Many physical and psychological disorders can be endured so long as one doesn't have to face. Flood, suffering as no cricketer should ever be asked to suffer, had the same idea.

Horace took guard. The delivery was the most downright Christian thing I've ever seen on a cricket pitch, but it was still beyond Horace's ability to lay a bat on it. The ball brushed his thigh with all the venom of a drugged moth and inched harmlessly towards the wicketkeeper.

'Come one!' screamed Blumenthal.

'Get back!' retorted Flood.

'We're running,' bawled Blumenthal and, to underline the point, hobbled towards the gully.

What could I do? My batsman had issued his instructions. His voice was the only one I listened to. So I ran. Bellflower, who was on the other side of the pitch, saw me go and ran, also. The wicketkeeper simply gaped. Bellflower and I completed our run, and turned.

'Stay!' shouted Blumenthal.

'Come one more!' bellowed Flood, so Bellflower did. I hesitated, as bidden, but incredibly the run seemed to be on, so I ran.

Only now the wicketkeeper picked up the ball. He threw it to silly mid-off, who threw it back to him. The keeper in turn threw it to the bowler, who missed it. Deep extra cover gathered it and threw it back to the wicketkeeper, who also missed it. Backward square leg picked it up, and hesitated. Second slip looked interested, so he threw it to him. Second slip caught it nicely, shied at the stumps, and missed them.

Mid-on stopped the ball and yet again returned it to the keeper.

All this took a while. Bellflower and I were pounding backwards and forwards, backwards and forwards, and must have run seven or eight. Finally the ball struck the umpire's foot and ricocheted onto the stumps. Somebody was out, Bellflower I think, though it didn't matter. Flood had left the pitch in tears, and Horace Blumenthal had finally become somebody else; Henry the Navigator, I believe. He was only a passable bowler, was Horace, but one hates to see any cricketer overcome by a personality change on the pitch. He was led away, which left Bellflower and me to complete the innings.

We scored 1 between us. It went down against Bellflower's name, but under the circumstances I think it should have been shared. I was run out – technically. I'd made my ground easily, but I've never argued with an umpire in my life.

Just after seven, two ambulances arrived to take us and our bags to the station. I couldn't honestly say I'd enjoyed my weekend, but it served to underline the fact that without the Laws cricket would be a mess, barely worth playing. That's something we should never forget.

For the curious, I attach the Bar Flies' scorecard:

C.P. Bartrum	Absent, incapacitated.	0
L. Smith	Absent, ill.	0
P.Q. O'Halligan	Absent, incapacitated.	0
M.N.P. Newbody	Absent, lost cap.	0
V. Hoskins	Retired, collapsed.	4
W.W. Flood	Retired, lachrymose.	4
C. Parsons	Hit wicket.	4
P.J. Harrison	*b*. Coddlington.	0

H. Blumenthal	Retired, change of personality.	0
J.A.P. Withers	Run out.	0
A. Bellflower	Not out.	1
Extras		8
	Total	21